# A CHRISTMAS KISS FOR THE HIGHLANDER

## Heart of a Scot, Book Nine
### *Second Edition*

# COLLETTE CAMERON

*Blue Rose Romance*®
*Portland, Oregon*

Sweet-to-Spicy Timeless Romance®

A CHRISTMAS KISS FOR THE HIGHLANDER
Heart of a Scot
Copyright © 2021 Collette Cameron®
Cover Art: Sheri McGathy

Attn: Permissions Coordinator
**Blue Rose Romance**®
8420 N Ivanhoe # 83054
Portland, Oregon 97203

eBook ISBN: 9781954307841
Print Book ISBN: 9781954307858

collettecameron.com

For Skye, he'd walk through molten lava.

His pride was as inconsequential as thistledown.

## Dedication

To everyone who loves
Christmas traditions, old and new.

*Eytone Hall, Scottish Highlands*
*September 1720*

Cantering his horse up the well-maintained drive to Eytone Hall, Quinn felt the tension easing from his muscles. It had always been like this when he visited Liam MacKay, Baron Penderhaven, one of the few men he called a true friend. One of the very few people he trusted. The doors to Eytone Hall were open to him whenever he decided to drop in for an unannounced visit, and today would be no exception.

He called no place home, preferring the freedom to come and go at will. But if he had, Eytone Hall came the closest. In fact, Liam's mother, Lady Penderhaven, made certain his usual chamber was always prepared and his clothes hung inside the wardrobe—clean.

"Thank ye." Handing Benedict's reins off to the liveried footman who'd hurried from the grand mansion to attend the gelding, Quinn skewed his mouth into a grin. It truly was good to be here.

He untied his pack from the saddle while sending his gaze around the familiar courtyard and lands. Creamy, shorn sheep dotted one sloping hillside, and reddish-brown Highland cows milled about on another.

Even he could admit there was something enjoyable about the familiarity and comfort of returning to a place where he'd known a degree of contentment and peace. *Contentment? Peace?* That was a stretch, and neither were things he'd particularly coveted.

Until recently.

Nevertheless, if he didn't relish his freedom so much, he might envy Liam MacKay. Slinging his pack over one shoulder, he drew his mouth into a grim line. No, he didn't. Liam had been through bloody hell these past few years.

"Simmons." He nodded to the austere butler poised beside the mansion's double doors. "Ye're lookin' well."

Simmons angled his hoary head. "As are ye, Mr. Catherwood." He closed the doors, then reached for Quinn's satchel. "I'll have yer bag delivered to yer usual chamber."

"Thank ye. Is Liam at home?" More than once, Quinn had arrived to find Liam absent, not that he wasn't still made wholly welcome by Lady Penderhaven and her daughter, Kendra. He'd known that minx since she'd worn braids, and she was still inevitably embroiled in some sort of mischief or other.

"Nae, he isna, though he is expected back any day." He passed Quinn's pack to the footman before angling toward the corridor. "Will ye join her ladyship for tea at half past three?"

Quinn would rather lick the marble floor than perch on a settee and exchange trivial comments, but he summoned a droll smile, nevertheless. He was capable of acting the part of a gentleman. After all, he'd been raised as such, even if he'd chosen to leave that life behind a decade ago.

What time was it, anyway?

His pocket watch had been rather smashed on his last mission, and he hadn't replaced the timepiece yet. He didn't relish cooling his heels in the salon for an hour or two, waiting for the lady of the house's arrival when he could traipse about outside or enjoy a long relaxing soak in the tub while sipping a glass of Liam's superior cognac.

"Lead on, good fellow. I shall endeavor to appear civilized." He clasped a palm to his chest. "I promise no' to slurp my tea or chew with my mouth open."

He might talk with his mouth full though.

One of Simmons' wiry eyebrows shied upward the merest bit. *Ah, that's right.* The butler didn't possess a sense of humor.

No one in Baron Penderhaven's household had ever accused Quinn of being ungentlemanly or, for that matter, of being a gentleman. He skirted the bounds of propriety, not quite drifting so far astray as to be ostracized but never teetering over the edge into complete respectability either.

"Might I suggest ye freshen up first?" Nothing subtle about that or the butler's slightly flared nostrils.

Quinn was quite covered in dust, and he stank of sweat and horse.

"Indeed. An excellent notion." He swiveled toward the impressive staircase instead.

Twenty minutes later, he tripped back down the risers, having made do with the washstand water after examining the night table clock and finding it three-quarters past two. Just his blasted luck, he'd also nicked himself shaving in his haste. Putting a fingertip to the still-stinging cut, he checked for fresh blood.

Wouldn't do to bleed all over his starched neckcloth. He only had three here.

He passed the impressive library and had nearly gone beyond the drawing room when movement inside the open doorway caught his attention. Scrunching his brows together into a puzzled frown, he halted.

Hadn't Simmons said tea was to be served in the rose salon?

No, although that was where her ladyship generally preferred to take her tea, the butler hadn't specified where earlier. Mayhap things had changed since Quinn last visited. After all, it had been over six months. He pivoted and, touching his cut again, strode into the room.

A startlingly exquisite woman with glorious, pale honey-colored hair piled atop her head and attired in a white and robin's egg blue gown whirled away from the window. Her incredibly blue eyes widened, and she put a delicate hand to her throat where a single row of creamy pearls rested.

A long, intense minute stretched out, lengthening into something extraordinary and potent as they stared at each other, neither seeming able to break the inexplicable and immediate powerful connection which thrummed between them.

*Good God.* He almost expected choruses of *Hallelujah* and the harmony of violin strings to fill the sweetly tense atmosphere.

Finally, somehow marshaling his composure, he swept into a gallant's bow. Not usually at a loss for words or one to falter when faced with something unexpected—after all, his line of work tossed him in the middle of the perilous and unforeseen on a daily basis—he commanded his galloping pulse to return to its normal pace.

Opening his mouth, he found every drop of moisture had vanished. He cleared his throat, then swallowed. Blast, he was behaving more ineptly than a wet-behind-the-ears pup.

She remained statue-still, much like a wary doe prepared to flee if he moved suddenly.

"Please permit me to introduce myself. Quinn Catherwood, yer most humble servant, my lady." He found himself standing over her, not consciously recalling having moved across the carpet. The top of her shiny head reached his shoulder.

He envisioned leading her in a dance, or wrapping his arms about her delicate shoulders, or resting his cheek on the crown of her head. Yes, to all of that and more.

The girl was impossibly more perfect up close, her skin milky and smooth as silk. Navy-blue ringed her light azure irises framed by golden, winged brows. A delicate floral and citrus scent wafted upward from her sleek hair, and he inhaled her heady fragrance.

She was… *Odin's teeth.* She was—God help him—an answer to a prayer he hadn't even known he'd desired. And she must be his. *His.*

Gazing up at him, her peach-tinted lips slightly parted, she seemed as transfixed as he. As if coming to her senses, she blinked and lowered her hand to her waist.

"I'm Skye Hendron, Baron Penderhaven's cousin, visiting from England," she said in a melodious, cultured tone. "I'm simply a miss, not a lady."

Very proper and English, but not the least stuffy or superior. Her voice held an unexpected husky quality that immediately sent his senses into a spin once more.

"I'm most pleased I decided to pay my auld friend a visit." Quinn couldn't drag his focus from her exquisite features or the lively intelligence dancing in her amused gaze.

*God's teeth.*

His pulse leaped again. An extended stay might be in order. No, most definitely was in order. "Will ye be here long?"

*God and all the saints, please say aye.*

A slight shadow passed over her features, tipping her lovely mouth downward as she directed her focus to the window behind him. "Truthfully, I'm not sure. My father has fallen ill, and my mother sent me to Eytone Hall while she tends him. I pray 'tis nothing serious." As if as an afterthought, she waved her hand gracefully. "Aunt Louisa is my mother's sister."

At her obvious distress, a strange coiling began in Quinn's middle, spreading outward until it tangled around his heart. How could he want to gather this woman in his arms and promise her she could rely upon him for…*what?*

Comfort? Protection? Security?

*Aye. Aye, and much more.*

Something he'd never considered until this very instant, but so wondrous that he'd be an absolute idiot not to pursue whatever *this* was.

"I'm sorry, lass. I'm sure ye'd rather be with them than here no' kennin' what is happenin'." He tipped his mouth into a compassionate arc. "It must weigh heavily on ye. Have ye any brothers or sisters?"

She pulled her vibrant gaze back, surprise and appreciation for his understanding shining in her eyes. "It does, and no. I am an only child."

So was he.

"Mr. Catherwood—"

"Quinn. Ye must call me Quinn, please. I would deem it the greatest honor."

Taking her soft hand in his, he cupped it reverently. How he wanted to hear his name on her lips. He didn't know what had come over him and, in truth, he didn't give a ragman's scorn. Something had clicked the instant he laid eyes upon her, and he knew as well as he knew his name that his life had inexplicably veered down a heretofore unexplored path.

It was terrifying. And exhilarating. And marvelous.

His request for her to address him by his given name lay completely outside the bounds of propriety, and yet she made no attempt to remove her hand from his. In fact, she cupped his palm back, her pale fingers in stark relief against his sun-browned skin. Her dainty, fine-boned hand nested inside his as if sculpted to fit there.

"And it would please me if you'd call me Skye," she said, a touch of color high on her cheekbones.

A secret thrill tunneled through him. She was bold in the sweetest way possible.

Eyes guileless and the merest bit curious, she curved her mouth upward. "Quinn, I know this may sound strange, and please believe me when I tell you I am not usually so forward, but I feel as if I've known you my entire life. That we aren't strangers meeting for the first time at all."

Yes, he knew exactly what she felt, because the same sensation sluiced through him.

She gave a self-conscious chuckle, and her lush lashes fanned against her porcelain skin for the space of a blink before she met his gaze again. A hint of becoming color tinged her sloping cheeks. "'Tis silly, I know."

"Nae, no' silly, Skye." He stepped nearer, drawing her close and then tipped her chin upward with one finger. "I ken exactly what ye mean, for though I canna explain it, I feel precisely the same way."

"You do?" she whispered, her breath sweet and smelling of strawberries.

"Aye, lass," he murmured before brushing his lips across the velvety softness of her fingers. "I feel like I've come home at last."

2

*One month later*

Despite the chilly October morning, Skye wandered the scrupulously maintained garden path. The last month had been both the most exciting and worrisome of her life.

Weeks ago, Quinn had arrived unannounced, quite tilting her world on end in a most delightful fashion. After enduring the worst thunderstorm she had ever experienced, Liam finally returned home with Emeline LeClaire. He'd saved her life during a flash flood, and they'd scandalously spent several days alone in a hunting lodge.

Skye quite thought it the most romantic thing.

One had only to look at them to see how in love they were.

Could everyone see how much she adored Quinn?

Was it as obvious as Liam and Emeline's affection for each other?

Lord, she hoped not. Chagrin nipped at her pride.

It was one thing to gaze at someone with admiration when one knew the sentiment was returned but quite another when no such words had passed between her and Quinn.

Shortly after Emeline's arrival, the entire household—she and Quinn included—had embarked on a great adventure. Well, at least Skye had thought it a great adventure. They'd journeyed to Edinburgh and, once there, Liam, Quinn, and several other Scots had foiled an assassination plot against dear Emeline.

She and Liam had married shortly after everyone's return to Eytone Hall.

Skye plucked a late-blooming aster blossom, fingering the delicate violet petals as she followed the meandering path.

*He loves me.*

*He loves me not.*

*He loves me.*

*He loves me not.*

She plucked the purple petals, one by one, a tiny smile arcing her mouth. There was no need for a flower to predict the outcome, for she was confident Quinn returned her regard.

A lone lavender blade extended from the aster's center.

*He loves me not.*

Frowning, her shoulders slumping, she exhaled deeply and tossed the spent blossom aside. *Flim flam.*

*He does care. I know he does.*

Her musings turned to the other matter plaguing her peace of mind.

Several days ago—was it close to a fortnight now?—Mama had written and explained the delay in Skye's returning home. Papa had taken a slight turn for the worse—nothing to fret over, she assured—but the two servants who'd also fallen ill were on the mend. The physicians were baffled at the nature of the lingering illness.

Skye expected to be bidden home any day. Unease niggled a trifle that she hadn't heard from her mother again, but no doubt caring for Papa was most time consuming.

A chuckle escaped her, and a dainty, greenish bird flitted away from the branch it perched upon.

A man accustomed to being active and constantly busy, her father wasn't a biddable patient, and Mama tended to fret overly much. Hence, why Skye had been trundled to her cousin's rather than risk her becoming ill too.

Though she missed her parents awfully—she'd never been apart from her mother before—she couldn't bear the notion of leaving Quinn. Even contemplating being apart from him brought hot, stinging moisture to her eyes.

When summoned, she must leave, of course. Even if he declared himself, she'd no choice but to return home. She adored her parents and wouldn't defy them. Quinn had never mentioned marriage. Perhaps he felt it was too soon.

It wasn't.

It didn't matter that she knew next to nothing about him. From the moment she'd seen him in the drawing room, fingering a small cut on his chin, her heart had been his. She couldn't find the words to express what had passed between them that day, but he'd been the attentive suitor since.

"There ye are," came a familiar melodious brogue.

How she loved Quinn's Scottish burr.

Not for the first time, he'd suddenly appeared as if thinking of him conjured him to her side. Unable to contain her joy, she smiled, extending her ungloved hand. "I was just thinking of you."

Waggling his eyebrows naughtily, he murmured seductively, "Indeed?" as he took her hand in his work-roughened palm.

"You are too cocky, by far." She adored how playful and easygoing he was.

A boyish grin quirked his molded mouth. "Have I told ye how beautiful ye are today?"

Laughing, she shook her head. "You tell me that every day, Quinn. You've praised my hair, nose, eyes, lips, skin, the size of my feet and hands, and my voice.

Though I know I am far from any such thing, you make me sound like a divine goddess or a vision of loveliness."

He made her feel like that too.

"'Tis true. I could gaze at ye forever and never grow tired. That shade of pink is especially becomin' on ye. It makes yer skin glow." Such warmth emanated from his pale green eyes that her toes curled.

Surely, he felt the same wild beating in his heart as she. The same yearning to see her when they were apart as she felt when away from him. She glanced behind him to the tall drawing room windows. Aunt Louisa stood framed behind the panes, and Skye reluctantly withdrew her hand. "My aunt watches us."

That was unusual. Normally, Aunt Louisa didn't fuss over Quinn's time with Skye. Skye had always presumed she trusted him, since he was such a good friend of Liam's.

To his credit, Quinn didn't glance over his shoulder but instead offered his arm. He gestured to the aster and then to the verdant meadows beyond the tailored gardens. "I'm pretendin' to expound upon the

Highland's many attributes," he said out the side of is mouth. "Nod as if I'm impartin' glorious knowledge to ye."

Choking on a giggle, Skye dutifully bobbed her head and pointed to another shrub.

He bent near, inspecting the fading foliage, going so far as to lift a branch. "I have nae idea whatsoever what this plant is or anythin' about it, except 'tis green."

"What shade of green?" she quipped. "Fern? Pine? Holly? Sage? Rosemary? Grass?"

A footman approached, his expression unusually grave. "Miss Skye, the dowager baroness requests yer presence in the rose parlor at once."

She exchanged a swift glance with Quinn. Was she to be chastised for permitting him to hold her hand too long? Summoning a smile, she said, "Of course. I shall come immediately."

He bowed and retreated.

"Please excuse me, Quinn."

"If ye'll permit me, Skye, I'll escort ye inside." He gave her a wicked wink. "It shall afford me a few more pleasurable moments in yer company."

"You are a flatterer, sir."

"Only with ye, lass." He pressed his hand atop her fingers that rested on his arm. "Only with ye."

How she wanted to believe that were true.

A few short minutes later, Skye entered the parlor.

Solemn-faced, Liam, Kendra, Emeline, and Aunt Louisa sat upon the matching settees. Were those tears in Aunt Louisa's and Kendra's gray eyes?

Liam promptly rose and came to meet her at the door. He took her elbow, kindness and something far more ominous glinting in his pewter eyes. "Come, Skye."

She tossed a glance over her shoulder into the corridor. She wanted Quinn. Whatever was about to happen, she wanted him at her side.

Hands on his hips, his neck bent, he listened to something Simmons whispered in his ear. Quinn jerked his head up, his gaze tangling with hers across the short distance. Devastation glimmered in his beautiful eyes. He mouthed her name just as Liam guided her farther into the room.

"Something is amiss," Skye said.

A statement of fact, not a question.

Liam and her aunt traded strained glances.

A nasty sense of dread curled around Skye's ribs, constricting her lungs and turning her cold from the inside out. She glanced to her aunt and each of her cousins in turn. "What is it? Tell me."

Her mouth bent upward into a wobbly smile, Aunt Louisa patted the cushion beside her. "Sit here, my dear."

Trepidation making her movements stiff, Skye sank onto the settee. Dread clawed at her stomach and bile rose in her throat.

At once, her aunt took her hand in hers, and Kendra flew to sit beside her. On the opposite settee, her eyes awash in tears, Emeline dropped her gaze to her lap. She swallowed hard and pursed her lips as if struggling not to cry.

"Skye…" Her aunt's eyelids drifted shut, and a fat droplet slid from the corner of her eye.

Genuine fear streaked down Skye's spine.

"What has happened? Is it Papa?" Had he taken

another turn for the worse, and that was why her mother hadn't written?

*Oh, God. Please. No.*

Tossing propriety aside, Liam sat upon the table. He leaned forward, his elbows resting on his knees, grief etched into the rugged planes of his face. "Skye, I am so verra sorry to have to tell ye that yer mother and father have succumbed to illness."

"Succumbed? Mama is ill too?"

"My darlin', yer father died nine days ago. Yer mother four," Aunt Louisa murmured, her voice strangled and tinny.

Skye blinked, then blinked again. A low buzzing began resounding in her ears. She shook her head to quell the annoying sound.

Aunt Louisa wrapped a comforting arm across her shoulders. "The two servants who'd fallen ill survived. The physicians suspected plague since yer father recently returned from France. But they've ruled that out. They canna be sure what the cause was but still believe yer father brought the illness home with him. And because yer mother tended him personally and didna protect her own health..."

Skye heard the gently uttered words, but her mind refused to believe the truth of them.

"No," she managed through stiff lips, wadding her skirts in her hands until her fingers cramped. "You're wrong. It's a mistake."

"Oh, Skye," whispered Kendra, her brogue thick and tortured as fat teardrops plopped onto her lap. "'Tis no'."

*No. No. No!*

"No!" Skye screamed, feeling as if her heart were being torn from her chest. "They cannot be dead," she sobbed, darting her gaze around the room in an effort to find an escape from this excruciating pain. "I…" A great rasping sob tore through her, the agony eviscerating. "I didn't get to say *goodbye.*"

Her breath stalled in her lungs, and she couldn't breathe. Spots flickered before her eyes.

She dragged her attention to the doorframe.

*Quinn.*

He strode into the room, his mouth pinched into a grave line.

With a soft cry, she collapsed into Aunt Louisa's side just as darkness claimed her.

## 3

Quinn waited outside Skye's chamber as he had every morning these past several days. He couldn't help but feel he'd overstayed his welcome at Eytone Hall. He'd arrived unannounced over two months ago and, until the past few days, he couldn't consider leaving.

Skye needed him.

By no means had she recovered completely from her parents' deaths. However, a tiny bit of color had returned to her smooth cheeks, and she'd begun to eat a mite more. Despite Liam's thunderous scowl of disapproval, Quinn had carried Skye to her chamber that awful day she'd learned of her parents' deaths.

He'd remained until the dowager baroness had shooed him out. For the next week, he'd taken up a vigil outside Skye's chamber. Several times, he'd persuaded Liam or her aunt to permit him inside.

Often, under the stringent eyes of her maid, he simply held Skye's hand and listened as she spoke of her childhood and her parents. Other times, he read to her, and he'd taken to haunting the kitchen to ask Mrs. Spence to prepare traditional British foods and dainties for Skye, which he made sure she ate a portion of.

He'd given her a week secluded in her chamber before he insisted she dress and venture to the drawing room. Her grief was overwhelming, but he refused to allow her to waste away from her sorrow.

Today, he had news he wished to share with her.

She'd not be happy, but he wanted her for his wife. Before he could ask Liam for her hand, he had personal business to attend to. He wouldn't speak to her of marriage before he left. After all, she would remain in mourning for some time.

He believed he could deal with all of the loose ends and return within a fortnight. Then he'd brave Liam's disapproval and contend for Skye's hand. It would've been much easier to approach Skye's father with the request to marry her.

*He* didn't know Quinn well.

Didn't know of his questionable past.

Liam did, however, and although they were the closest of chums, Liam disapproved of Quinn as husband material for his cousin, now also his ward.

Skye emerged from her chamber and, as always, she offered him a fragile smile.

"Good morrow to ye, Skye."

*My dear one. My heart. The light of my formerly blasé life. My reason for risin' from my bed each mornin' and for each breath I inhale.*

She'd entranced him from the moment they'd met, but her smile had sealed his love and devotion for all time. He knew with everything in him that if he couldn't take Skye to wife, he'd never marry.

Her somber black gown rustling softly about her trim ankles, she placed her long, delicate fingers in the curve of his elbow. "Good morning."

"I have a surprise for ye." He smiled down into her eyes, memorizing her entrancing features. The slope of her cheeks. The arch of her brows. Her bowed lips. "Do ye want it now or after we break our fast?"

She cut him an amused, slightly reproving glance. "You cannot tell me you have a surprise for me and then expect me to wait until after I've eaten to discover what it is."

He chuckled, drawing her nearer his side. Her delicate fragrance rose to his nostrils. "We'll need to venture belowstairs."

With a bit more spring in her step than there had been for ages, Skye accompanied him to the orderly kitchens.

"Good mornin', Mrs. Spence. Is that item in the larder still?" he asked, glancing about the tidy space.

Herbs hung from several hooks, and someone had been busy baking, though the day was young. A long table near the window held a dozen loaves of bread, four pies, and two types of biscuits. If he wasn't mistaken, one was shortbread.

He practically salivated from the delicious smells permeating the large room.

Mrs. Spence, her face ruddy and tinged with moisture, turned from the stove. "Aye, Mr.

Catherwood." A twinkle entered her kind eyes and she smiled, her cheeks forming plump apples. "I think Miss Skye will be mighty pleased."

On impulse, he asked, "Would it be a huge imposition to request breakfast trays for Miss Skye and me in the drawin' room, rather than us eatin' in the breakfast room this mornin'?"

The cook cut a knowing glance to the closed larder door. "Nae problem at all. I'll have them sent up after ye leave."

"Whatever are you about, Quinn?" A brightness lit Skye's stunning blue eyes that he hadn't seen in weeks.

He'd cut off his right hand to see that glow of happiness there every day.

"Come." He took her hand and drew her to the larder. He cautiously opened the door, then poked his head inside. Giving her a wide grin, he shoved the door wide and gestured for her to precede him.

She stepped inside and gasped. Lying on a folded blanket, its tiny paws covering its nose, lay a long-haired calico kitten. "Oh, Quinn," Skye breathed, rushing forward and dropping onto her knees. She gathered the sleeping kitten into her arms. "Hello there, darling."

The kitten blinked citrine eyes and yawned widely before reaching her paw out to bat at one of the fair curls over Skye's ear.

"She's adorable," Skye declared after checking the multi-colored little furball's sex.

Quinn extended a hand to help her up.

Cradling the tiny kitten to her chest, she rose, her eyes shining. "Thank you. She's simply precious."

He stepped nearer, so close Skye's lips were but inches away. He'd forbidden himself such delicious liberties until they were formally betrothed. Now he cursed his chivalry to the devil. Instead of kissing her as he yearned to do, he brushed a bent finger over her velvety cheek. Pray someday, he'd have the right to touch all of her silky skin.

"What will ye name the wee mite?"

As she often did when thinking or considering, she scrunched her nose slightly. Head canted, she ran a finger down the kitten's spine which earned her a blink, and the softest purring Quinn had ever heard began.

"Why, I don't know," Skye said. "I've never named an animal before. Have you any suggestions? Her coat is so colorful, like a patchwork quilt."

He bent his neck, examining the kitten he'd rescued yesterday afternoon when he'd ventured to the village to post a series of letters. "She has a black patch over her eye."

"Patches." Skye glanced up, grinning. "I'll call her Patches."

His breath stuttered behind his ribs at the joy radiating on her face. "Perfect."

Ten minutes later, they sat on the carpet before the hearth in the drawing room playing with Patches. Skye had snipped a length of yarn from her aunt's knitting basket and trailed it back and forth across the floor. Patches leaped and bounced in pursuit of the pale pink wool.

"I thought she could keep ye company," Quinn said. He was leaving Eytone Hall this morning.

Skye swiftly raised her head, her acute gaze

searching his. "You're leaving?"

He couldn't miss the distress in her eyes or tone.

A footman and a maid entered carrying the breakfast trays, and she directed her attention to the frolicking kitten.

"Where would ye prefer these, Miss Skye? Mr. Catherwood?" the footman asked.

Skye indicated the table between the two sofas. "There will be fine. Thank you."

The maid smiled and pointed to a bowl. "Mrs. Spencer sent a spot of milk along for the wee kitten. There's a bit of diced chicken for her too."

"Please tell her thank you. That was most thoughtful." Skye's perfect manners didn't quite hide her upset.

At least not from Quinn. He doubted the servants took any notice.

With a bow and a curtsy, the footman and maid departed.

Quinn angled to his feet, then offered his hand to assist Skye. When she stood before him, he drew her near, her chest almost touching his.

A crease pulling her fair eyebrows together, she stared at his cravat. She was upset.

"I shall be back, Skye." He tilted her chin up, his heart squeezing at the sadness she tried valiantly to disguise. "I promise, I shall. In a fortnight."

She averted her gaze and swallowed before bringing her eyes back to his. "You will be careful? I should hate for anything to happen to you."

"Aye, my precious English lass. Most careful. Nothing can keep me from ye. I vow it."

"Ahem," Simmons cleared his throat. "Yer mount is ready and waitin', Mr. Catherwood."

Skye stepped away, putting a respectable distance between them. With her usual grace, she swept to the table and removed the dome from a plate. Patches romped after her, swatting at her swaying skirts.

Quinn inclined his head. "Thank ye, Simmons. I'll be there shortly."

"Verra good, sir." The butler withdrew.

"You won't eat first?" She gestured at the food.

"Nae. The sooner I'm away, the sooner I can return to ye." In three strides, he was at her side. He took her hand and lifted it to his lips, pressing a fervent kiss to her knuckles. If only he dared kiss her sweet mouth, but he'd do nothing to stir Liam's disapproval or wrath.

Her lips trembled, but she fashioned a brave smile. "I shall miss you."

"And I ye." *My darling, love.*

He was off to do something he'd vowed never to do as long as he drew a breath: Claim his inheritance.

4

*9 December 1720*

Exhaling a dejected breath, Skye released the heavy drapery festooning Eytone Hall's tall library window. With a gentle swoosh, the claret-colored velvet settled into place once more. The starless winter sky and perfectly symmetrical hedges veiled the courtyard and any misplaced hope of spying a newly arrived coach.

*His coach.*

What she'd believed was the crunching of gravel beneath wheels on the drive had awoken her, and she'd darted to the window, anticipation and joy sluicing through her.

*He's back. He's back. Quinn is back!*

Still half-asleep, she'd flung the drapery aside and pressed her nose to the icy glass, straining to see…anything.

She must've been dreaming. Again. He'd rode away atop a horse, but it wasn't improbable he'd return by coach. Was it?

For the fifth night in a row, nestled on the divan and trying to read *Robinson Crusoe*—a Christmas gift from Papa last year—she'd dozed off while waiting for Quinn's return. How pathetic did that make her? Waiting in vain, night after night?

The novel helped to keep her mind occupied and her thoughts from straying to her parents' untimely deaths less than a week apart. Quinn's solicitous presence at Eytone Hall had made their passing a trifle more bearable.

*Only just.*

Quinn, Liam, Kendra, Aunt Louisa, and Emeline had all been wonderfully considerate and compassionate in her time of sorrow.

What would she have done without them?

Nonetheless, she missed Quinn intolerably.

Those first few awful days when she'd functioned in a fog of disbelief and numbness, he'd been her rudder, providing her with his much-needed strength, stability, and reassurance. He'd encouraged her to eat, though she had no appetite, and gently insisted she take innumerable strolls around the house, the terrace, and the gardens when the tetchy autumn weather permitted.

He'd even contrived to present her with Patches. From whence he'd procured the kitten, she had no idea, but she'd fallen in love with the fluffy darling at once. Even now, the needle-clawed bundle of mischief snoozed contentedly on the divan Skye had vacated.

Something spontaneous, wonderful, and unnamable—*magical, even*—had sprung up between her and Quinn from the moment they'd met that day in September, and she'd honestly believed...

*It doesn't matter. It's over. He left, and he's obviously not coming back.*

Disappointment crested in her breast, tightening her throat, and tears stung behind her eyelids. Tears she refused to shed. By heavens, she was done with weeping!

Yet, for several labored breaths, hopelessness and loneliness overwhelmed, shrouding her in gloom. Lower lip clamped between her teeth and hands fisted in the skirts of her gown, she rested her forehead against the velvet panel, struggling not to yield to the grief that was her ever-present companion these past several weeks.

A chill swept over her despite her simple, black woolen gown and layers of petticoats, and a shiver scuttled across her shoulders and down her spine, puckering her flesh. The weather had turned bitingly cold and unrelentingly windy a week ago. 'Twas a wonder snow didn't cloak the Highlands.

"Brr." Briskly rubbing her arms, Skye doubted she'd ever feel warm again. Truly warm and toasty. And content.

England's perpetual shrapnel-colored skies, damp, and fog were trifling nuisances, much like a pebble in one's shoe, compared to the Highland's brusque, uncompromising clime. But it was the icy deadness in her heart that chilled her to her marrow—that stole her hope.

She dreaded never shaking her despair and that at nineteen years of age, this frigid, unyielding ache that had taken up residence in her soul would last forever. This moroseness would insidiously and stealthily become her new normal, until she forgot the gay, optimistic woman she'd been before her parents' deaths.

Before Quinn left, vowing to return to her.

Turning from the elegant row of windows, she continued rubbing her arms as she crossed to the divan. She picked up the navy-blue, gold-lettered leather book which had tumbled to the parquet floor in her haste. Once she'd set it on the rosewood end table, she gathered the delicate ivory shawl off the divan and rubbed it against her cheek.

*Mama made this.*

Knowing her mother's hands had knitted the delicate covering, Skye took great comfort in wrapping herself in the soft wool.

Patches opened her eyes for a sleepy, amber-eyed blink before tucking her half-pink, half-black nose underneath her white-tipped paws once more.

Draping the wrap over her shoulders, Skye wandered to the fireplace and stared into the soothing yellow and orange flames.

A weary glance to the tortoise shell Louis XIV Religieuse clock revealed half past eleven.

She ought to seek her bed.

Except, she knew as well as she knew her name was Skye Arabella Louisa Hendron that sleep would evade her until the wee morning hours when physical exhaustion toppled her into a restless, weird, dream-filled slumber. She'd awake a few hours later to leaden eyelids, gritty eyes, and a head which felt full of wet wool.

Thoughts of Quinn, adjusting to her life in the Highlands as Liam's ward, the sudden and unexpected deaths of her parents, and what her future held tumbled around and around *and around* in her mind as she tried to sleep. To forget, if only for a little while.

In recent days, she'd been sorely tempted several times to dose herself with the laudanum the doctor had prescribed when she'd collapsed upon learning she'd been orphaned.

*Papa had been recovering so well, and then—*

Skye would like to think she was made of sterner stuff; that the bitter medicine didn't entice her to dull her pain. After all, she was half-Scots, and a heartier, more stoic people didn't exist. But she'd been raised in Wigginton as a gentle-bred Englishwoman, and it was so very hard to appear brave and strong when her life crumbled apart around her.

So far, she'd resisted the gentle urgings to seek the temporary reprieve the laudanum would provide. Facing her troubles with a sharp mind and acute senses was preferable.

Sighing again, she flexed her shoulders, a brittle half-smile arcing her mouth as her musings turned to Quinn once more.

Quinn Catherwood…as mysterious as he was striking, and the man who'd unknowingly captured her heart in the few short weeks since they'd met. *Bah.* He'd captured her heart that very first day.

When the light caught his sandy-brown hair just so, distinct golden-bronze hues appeared. Lashes a much darker brown than his hair framed green eyes so pale as to be almost colorless.

Eyes containing gold flecks and a gray-blue ring around the iris, and the slightest creases at the corners. Eyes that had flashed with mirth and, she'd been so certain, gazed at her with something more than affection. A remarkable man whose heady, outdoorsy, spicy scent she could almost smell if she closed her eyes and concentrated.

Not overly tall—he stood but four or five inches over her own five-foot seven height—he was sinewy and strong, exuding power, charm, and self-confidence. He wasn't arrogant but simply a man comfortable with himself. One who didn't strive to impress others or care excessively what people thought of him. He was unerringly kind and quite funny too. And so very tender and considerate.

Every detail about him was etched into her spirit for all time.

Kissing her knuckles and holding her hand far longer than was proper, he'd promised to return to Eytone Hall in less than a fortnight. With a cocky salute, he'd lithely swung into the saddle atop Benedict three and twenty days, fifteen hours, and thirty-seven minutes ago.

She was a naive ninny to have expected him to actually return to Eytone Hall. To her.

Liam's not so subtle caution that Quinn was a libertine, a *roué,* who called no place home and whose precise occupation was somewhat murky had gone unheeded. For she'd blithely gone and done what so many gullible young girls had before her; she'd allowed her head to be turned and her heart ensnared by a rake and a rogue. More fool she.

*But an oh so wonderfully, devilish Highland rogue.*

Quinn was also a true gentleman. He'd never once pushed the bounds of propriety and tried to steal a kiss or made improper innuendos. *More's the pity.*

Mouth pursed, and vexed with her own naïveté, she shrugged, at last acknowledging the truth she'd strived to deny.

Quinn wasn't coming back.

He'd only been kind to a young, enamored girl with stars in her eyes who was mourning her parents' passing. And though he might've enjoyed their innocent flirtation, a worldly man about town such as Quinn Catherwood wasn't interested in settling down in England or Scotland and marrying a successful merchant's daughter.

Or any woman, for that matter, Liam had advised her with a good measure of compassion but also the brutal frankness that was his way.

Never had a Christmas season—Skye's favorite time of the year until now—loomed as dismal and dreary. She wrinkled her nose and skimmed a glance over the well-kept room. Why, the Scots didn't even celebrate the occasion due to some antiquated law or decree.

How could she bear December and all of the memories of Christmases past without Mama and Papa? Without the church service to celebrate Christ's birth? The decorations and music and Yule log and delicious foods? The gifts for the less fortunate?

How—*God and all the angels*—could she bear it without Quinn?

*Oh, Quinn, my love.* If he were here, the season

might hold a degree of joy after all. But he wasn't and there was nothing—

*Wait a minute.*

Mayhap…yes, mayhap, she could ask Liam and Aunt Louisa if they'd permit her a few Christmas traditions. It would certainly steer her mind from woeful musings and might even cheer her a measure. Scooping Patches into her arms and nuzzling the kitten's soft fur, she smiled as she retrieved the book as well.

Yes, that's exactly what she'd do.

Plan a Highland Christmas celebration and cease spending her evenings waiting in vain in the library.

## 5

Quinn squinted at the moonless sky as he tromped along, leading his lame horse. He'd forsworn the comfort of coach travel and the luxury of luggage for expediency. In his haste to reach Skye, he hadn't taken the care for Benedict as he should've either.

Now the poor beasty suffered because of his foolhardiness. He slowed his pace and patted the horse's neck. "Sorry I am, laddie. Ye ken I'd never deliberately bring harm to ye."

The faithful creature pushed his shoulder. Benedict had been the only thing, other than the clothes on his back, Quinn had taken when he'd left home a decade ago as a lad of seventeen.

His heavy woolen coat, hat, scarf, and gloves did little to keep the angry, determined wind from seeping into his garments and freezing his very bones. His limbs felt leaden from fatigue and cold, and only the knowledge of what awaited him at his destination kept him trudging forward, one plodding foot in front of the other.

Too blasted bad that, unlike Liam, he didn't tote a flask of whisky in his pocket, or he'd take a hearty nip this very minute.

Delayed several days in London and then almost a week in Edinburgh, he was long overdue at Eytone Hall. He supposed he could've written Skye but, truth be told, he'd likely arrive before the letter did, such was the inconsistency and slowness of the post boys and the public postal service.

*Skye.*

So named for the Isle of Skye by her homesick mother, Skye had informed him with her usual candor. Just thinking of her warmed his innards, causing a sweet sensation similar to premium aged scotch to heat his blood and belly.

Her brilliant eyes, as bright and clear azure-colored as a summer morning, sparkled with mischief and delight, and her hair, laced with threads of gold and champagne, formed a silky blonde halo around her exquisite oval face.

He adored the way she wrinkled her pert nose in concentration and longed to touch his mouth to her berry-red lips that he'd barely resisted kissing for so many tormenting weeks.

*Och, aye. My bonnie, braw Skye.*

He'd known from that first devastating—slightly bashful—smile that blossomed across her dewy face that sunny September afternoon that he'd met his soulmate. Until that moment, he didn't believe in such codswallop and numpty twaddle. He'd never jeer or mock another person or call them a clot head about love again. For when Cupid's arrow had unerringly struck him, he fell completely, recklessly, and irrevocably in love with Skye Hendron.

A loud, scornful snort escaped him, creating a miniature cloud before his face in the frigid air.

Him—Quinn Broc Steaphan Catherwood—a loner with no family of his own other than his maternal grandmother, and a wanderer with no place he called home, except for the hospitality and benevolence of his friends, Liam MacKay and Broden McGregor, was hopelessly in love.

Enamored. Enthralled. Utterly besotted with an Englishwoman. *Half-English.* Her mother had been Scots, the sister of Louisa MacKay, the Dowager Baroness Penderhaven.

Nearby, something scurried away, rustling the bushes and causing Benedict to shake his head and sidestep.

"Easy, lad. Just a rabbit or a mouse. No' too much farther." Another hour or so.

Wild horses couldn't have torn Quinn away from Skye after her parents' tragic deaths. But in the tranquil weeks that followed, he'd appreciated he must put his affairs to rights and become above reproach. *If* he wanted to make her his own for all time and stood any chance of Liam accepting his offer for her hand.

Friend or not, Liam had made his feelings very clear about his cousin. She was off-limits to Quinn's romantic pursuit, and he wouldn't welcome his addresses, longtime friend or not. Actually, they were more like the brother neither had. Nonetheless, he knew Liam well enough to not doubt he'd meant what he'd said about Skye.

Quinn—Liam had said with his typical candor—wasn't up to par by any stretch of anyone's imagination.

Well, the *old* Quinn certainly wasn't a model gentleman.

This newly reformed, upright denizen of society might be acceptable. By God, he'd be so pious, respectable, and decent, all of the saints—and even the Pope himself—would gaze upon him with a benign smile of approval.

Before meeting Skye, he would've sworn he'd perish from boredom if required to become upright, but a life with her made the possibility something to look forward to rather than dread. "Nothin' I wouldna do for ye, my Skye," he murmured into the blustery winter air.

His self-castigating chuckle rent the December night's peaceful stillness, and Benedict twitched his ears, giving him a reproving look with his big brown eyes that said, "Have ye lost yer bloody mind?"

Quinn chuckled again, never having felt more alive and full of optimism. Liam might take some convincing. *Nae, he'll bloody well take a great deal of convincin'.* After all, he was intimately acquainted with Quinn. Knew things about him no one else did.

He knew the Quinn of old.

Not the Quinn in love with Skye.

The Quinn, who after ten years of refusing a single farthing of his inheritance, had swallowed the boulder of pride lodged in his throat and decided to accept his legacy. He'd also called upon his mother's mother, Elspet Dunwoodie. Every bit as proud and stubborn as Quinn, Grandmama was granddaughter to an earl and Quinn's only remaining blood relation.

It had been almost a year since he'd last seen her, having left her drawing room on a tide of frustrated anger when she'd, yet again, suggested he was a pig-headed Scot for refusing his legal bequeathment. He couldn't let her know the godawful truth though.

Aye, he might've been lawfully entitled to the fortune, but the means by which his father, and his before him, accrued the other portion of the familial wealth disgusted Quinn to his core. Both were men of such immoral repute that he'd seriously considered changing his surname to distance himself further from their foulness.

They boasted to everyone who inquired—and many who hadn't—that investments in rum and sugar had enhanced their already solid financial dynasty. That piece of their tale, spun to reflect upon them favorably, contained a degree of truth. However, what they failed to mention was the other, much more profitable and scurrilous, way they'd filled their coffers.

Home early from university, he'd ventured into his father's office to request foolscap and ink to respond to an invitation to a house party. Unexpectedly finding the room empty, during his search for paper, Quinn had accidentally stumbled upon a journal of sorts atop his sire's desk.

The record not only detailed the kidnapping and transporting of children and poverty-stricken and indebted adults by ship to the colonies, but also selling them as indentured servants. The macabre diary detailed rapes and other assaults, victims killing themselves, and the horrific punishments inflicted upon any who resisted or tried to flee.

Without a word or his father ever knowing he'd been there, he'd left. He'd never returned home, and he never saw his father or grandfather again. What he had done was send them a single letter telling them precisely why he'd severed relations with them.

When the solicitor contacted him to inform him of his father's death and his subsequent bequeathment, he'd mourned the latter more than the former. Quinn had expected to be disinherited. Disowned.

Even now, a decade later, bile burned the back of his throat at the atrocities they committed for coin, and nausea churned his stomach that their putrid blood flowed in his veins.

That was why as a member of a highly secret— *illegal*—society, he'd dedicated his life, up to this point, to the extermination of forced labor, slavery, and indentured servitude.

But such a life was too dangerous for a married

man. Hadn't he nearly been killed half a dozen times? Nevertheless, he'd find other methods to continue the fight to help the oppressed.

As a respectable man of means with connections, he'd have the power to influence people. Profiting from the suffering of others was unconscionable and it must be put to a stop.

Truthfully, he never believed the day would come that he'd put aside his fury and hatred of his father and grandfather. But for Skye, he'd walk through molten lava. His pride was as inconsequential as thistledown.

Yes, to make her his bride, he'd willingly, eagerly, cease his wild recklessness and cede his wanderlust, for he'd finally found a home. In the heart of the most remarkable, extraordinary woman to grace God's beautiful earth.

Skye Hendron.

He directed his attention overhead just as the clouds broke, and the moon's silvery glow burst through. Almost like a good omen. A derisive grin tilted his mouth on one side. Since when did he believe in such nonsensical claptrap?

Nonetheless, he closed his eyelids and sent up a most fervent and sincere silent prayer that he'd be blessed with his greatest desire. Since he was turning over a new leaf, now was as good a time as any, he supposed, to explore the faith in the Almighty who Skye was so committed to.

Humming a rather ribald ditty, he raised his collar higher against the mercilessly cutting wind and, hunching into his coat, tramped onward. Given the moon's position, he guessed the time to be well past midnight. Rather rude and inconsiderate of him to arrive at Eytone Hall in the middle of the night, but he couldn't wait one more day to see Skye.

Besides, he'd passed by the last posting house miles ago.

Quinn wouldn't wake the household, however. As he'd done numerous times prior, he'd enter through the kitchens and find his way to his room. It wouldn't be the first time the MacKays, or the McGregors either, had sat down to break their fast and he'd wandered in to greet them.

He quite enjoyed the astonishment on their faces.

However, his days of trotting about and being accountable to no one but himself and his superior were over. Yet an unpleasant thought he couldn't dismiss had dogged him for days and now pulled his eyebrows together in a fierce scowl. *God's bones.* Given his delay, Skye might think he'd lied to her. That he had no intention of returning. There'd been no help for his tardiness though.

After visiting Grandmama, and the tough old bird skillfully extracting a promise he'd bring Skye to meet her, he'd called upon his father's solicitor and then The Royal Bank of Scotland.

He was a wealthy man.

Wealthier than he'd initially believed. The knowledge didn't fill him with satisfaction. Except, the monies might persuade Liam that Quinn was a good match for Skye after all, and that he wasn't a fortune hunter. The funds also put him in a position financially to assist those unfortunate souls without the ability to help themselves.

His final appointment had been with his superior to submit his resignation. He'd reluctantly received permission to return to civilian life after he accomplished one last mission. That task was completed yesterday afternoon, and two lads—not more than eight years old—had been spared indentured servitude in the colonies. With only the merest regret, he'd bid his old life goodbye.

Quinn, the covert operative, was no more.

## 6

The next morning, Skye awoke surprisingly refreshed and with a sense of anticipation bubbling behind her breastbone. Laying amongst the comfy pillows, Patches curled contentedly and purring at her side, she contemplated her newfound optimism.

*Christmas in the Highlands.*

Yes, that was what had sparked the expectancy in her.

Last night, she'd decided to see if Liam would permit her a Christmas at Eytone Hall. She rather assumed he wouldn't deny her request. He'd been as concerned as Aunt Louisa, Kendra, and Emeline about her doldrums. And she also suspected he knew she harbored warm sentiments for Quinn.

Compassion and sympathy for her parents' deaths

was to be expected, but she couldn't bear Liam's pitying looks. A flush warmed her, but she dismissed her discomfiture. Diving into holiday preparations would give her something to do and keep her mind occupied. The very thing she'd needed most to keep her riotous thoughts corralled.

Other than Quinn, of course.

With a renewed sense of vigor, and more energy than she'd had in weeks, she flung back the bedclothes much to Patches' disconcertment. The kitten leaped to her feet, arched her back, and hissed.

At once, Skye apologized. "I'm sorry, darling. I didn't mean to frighten you."

Soothing the miffed feline, she lifted Patches from the gold, ivory, and robin's egg blue coverlet. After a few more murmured words of comfort and much petting, Skye set her down on a favorite pillow. With promises of special treats from the kitchen, she attended to her toilette with alacrity that surprised even her.

She truly anticipated something for the first time in months. Something besides Quinn's return, that was.

Mentally making a list of her favorite Christmas traditions and the supplies that would need procurement, Skye dressed in another plain black gown, twisted her waist-length hair into a loose knot at the back of her head, and dabbed perfume behind each ear and at her wrists. Wrinkling her forehead at her much-too-somber attire, she eyed her jewelry box.

*Why not?*

'Twas the season to be festive, was it not?

In the wake of donning her mother's emerald and pearl earbobs, she examined herself in the rosewood cheval mirror. Still rather drab, especially her pale cheeks. She pinched the too-wan flesh and, before she could think on it overly much, clasped an emerald brooch to her bodice before entwining a length of matching ribbon in her hair.

Sitting on the end of the bed, watching her every move, Patches meowed and appeared to nod.

"You approve?" Skye eyed herself in the mirror once more.

*Yes, much better.*

She brushed her fingertips over her black skirts and pulled her mouth into a straight line. She'd adored wearing burgundy or midnight blue or green or silver or gold during Twelfth Night, but it was too soon to toss off her mourning weeds.

She twisted her mouth into a rueful smile. Truth to tell, she generally started wearing holiday colors the first week in December. Mama used to say, "I declare, my darlin' wee lass, nobody loves Christmastide more than ye."

Feeling slightly mischievous—it had been so long since she had—she seized another length of wider ribbon. Soon, Patches bore a bright red bow. She gave Skye the gimlet eye, not at all pleased with the frippery. Her plaintive yowl only earned her a sympathetic quirk of Skye's lips.

"You'll become accustomed to the ribbon, darling. Christmas comes but once a year, and you must look the part too." Cradling the cat in one arm, she left the bedchamber.

~*~

A few minutes later, seated at the cozy table in the breakfast room, a bowl of porridge before her, Skye bit her lip, suddenly unsure the Christmas idea would be met with any degree of enthusiasm.

After all, what was an annual tradition for her wasn't celebrated by anyone here. Her family couldn't miss what they'd never known and might think her silly for wanting to recreate the event at Eytone Hall.

As they were wont to do every morning, Aunt Louisa, Kendra, and Emeline chatted about their plans for the day. Liam looked on, a tolerant slant to his mouth. He'd escape to his study or the outdoors before long, Prince—his huge, raggedy dog of questionable heritage—at his side.

She hid a grin as Liam, wholly straight-faced, slid a hand beneath the tablecloth and the entire table wobbled. No one so much as blinked as Prince wolfed down his not-so-secret morsel.

Needing a bit of fortification before she introduced her wild idea to the others, Skye took a drink of cooled tea from the saucer. She'd rehearsed what she wanted to say to convince Liam and Aunt Louisa to permit her the festivities. Naturally, she'd cover the cost, and she'd keep the merriments low-key and unostentatious.

"How did ye sleep, Skye? Well, I do hope." Also attired in mourning black, with the addition of a dainty black lace cap atop her neatly arranged sable curls, Aunt Louisa eyed Skye fondly as she spread berry preserves on her bread. "Ye seem in a little better spirits today."

Except for her dark hair and gray eyes—*Mama possessed gray-blue eyes and almost blonde hair*—Aunt Louisa greatly resembled her younger sister. She sounded exactly like her, however. More than once, Skye had momentarily thought she heard her mother speaking before reality unmercifully crashed down upon her.

"I did sleep quite well." The best night's rest she'd had in months, truth be told. "Very well, indeed, actually. I had a thought last night..." She had everyone's attention now. Clearing her throat, she patted her mouth then, gathering her initiative, and draped her serviette across her gown once more. "I know 'tisn't customary in Scotland, but I wondered, perhaps, if we mightn't celebrate Christmastide this year?"

Kendra sat up straighter, a distinct glint of interest and excitement in her dove-gray eyes. "Och, could we? I've read about the festivities. It sounds so grand and entertainin'. I'd love to make a clove orange pomander."

Unusually restrained, she swept her gaze expectantly between her brother and mother.

Emeline beamed, catching her husband's eyes, and a slow smile kicked up one side of Liam's mouth. His bride colored prettily, a matching smile framing her lips.

Skye was quite certain the current discussion had absolutely no bearing on his joviality or his wife's demureness.

"It would be such good fun, Liam," Kendra said, her enthusiasm contagious.

Aunt Louisa set her knife on her plate and, slanting her head slightly, regarded Skye intensely. "Och, that explains the red bow Patches is wearin'. I thought perhaps ye were tryin' to keep tabs on the little beasty."

Unfortunately, Patches had a penchant for

pouncing on Aunt Louisa's ankles and making mischief in her yarn basket. She'd also left a dead mouse, it's four tiny feet poking straight upward, atop the cushion of Aunt Louisa's favorite chair in the salon.

Skye hadn't been able to convince Aunt Louisa that meant Patches liked her. Cats only brought *gifts* to those they favored and wanted to share with, she'd explained. Aunt Louisa had sniffed and declared she was loath to contemplate what Patches might bring should she dislike her.

Waving her fingers, Skye indicated her earrings and brooch. "These are my first small attempts at seasonal gayness, since mourning rather limits me presently."

Approval shone in her aunt's kind gaze. "They are lovely on ye."

Not receiving any immediate objections to her idea, she rushed on, "I know the holiday isn't widely observed in Scotland, but Mama and Papa always celebrated in England." Skye's father had been an Englishman through and through, though he disdained drunken revelry. "It has always been my favorite time of year, and I thought, perhaps, by including a few of the simpler traditions, I mightn't miss them quite so much this year…"

She trailed off as she voiced the pain squeezing her heart.

"Och, well, now." Liam leaned forward, speculation glinting in his eyes, the same quicksilver shade as Kendra's. Fingering the handle of his knife, he dipped his chin in a contemplative nod. "'Tisn't illegal, per se."

"What's no' illegal?"

Everyone swung their astounded attention to the entry. Bold as brass and wearing an equally bright smile, Quinn strode into the breakfast room, his gaze immediately fastening on Skye.

She barely suppressed a cry of delight.

*He came! Oh, thank the divine powers. Quinn is here.*

Prince woofed a warning and trotted to greet him. After circling and sniffing quite intrusively around Quinn's ankles and bum, he padded back to Liam.

Kendra slipped him a bite of egg as he passed, and he wagged his bushy tail in thanks.

If everyone kept feeding the dog, he'd be as round as a goat expecting triplets before long.

"Christmas 'tisn't illegal," Skye managed, sounding almost normal. Difficult to do with glee burbling behind her ribs and delight toppling her stomach over on itself. "We're to have a Christmas at Eytone Hall this year." She slid a quick glance to Liam. "That is, if Liam approves."

Even if he said no, the only thing she wanted for Christmas stood framed in the entry as virile and handsome as she'd remembered.

Why had he come back?

Because he'd promised to?

Or was there another reason?

It was all Quinn could do to keep himself from striding across the carpet, scooping Skye into his arms, and kissing her until they both grew dizzy.

Or Liam punched him.

She looked impossibly more fetching than the last time Quinn had seen her three and a half weeks ago. Color blossomed across her sculpted ivory cheeks as she gifted him a beatific smile. He'd have walked across Scotland barefoot in January to see the luster of her incandescent smile directed toward him like that.

Even her drab ebony gown couldn't detract from her loveliness. She'd deemed to wear gems today, so hopefully that meant she was starting to heal from her parents' deaths. He'd be right by her side from now on to make certain she didn't have to do so alone anymore.

Liam surged to his feet and came around the table. He clasped Quinn's hand in a hearty grip and slapped his shoulder. "'Tis good to see ye. When did ye arrive?"

"Early this mornin'. I believe 'twas about quarter past three." He glanced out the north-facing, frost-etched window to the stables beyond. "My horse went lame, forcin' me to walk the last several miles. I didna want to disrupt the household so late, so I used the kitchen entrance."

"But 'twas freezin' last night." Eyes wide, Kendra looked aghast. "Ye might've froze."

"She's right, Quinn. More than one Highlander has unexpectedly met his maker by underestimatin' the frigid temperatures," the Dowager Baroness Penderhaven said, adding a lump of sugar to her tea. "Why didna ye travel by coach?"

"Horseback is much faster." He cast Skye a meaningful glance and was pleased to see her blue eyes widen in understanding and a tinge of pink sprout upon her cheeks. "Besides, I'm accustomed to the elements, and I really didna have any choice once Benedict went lame. We either kept goin' or spent the night outdoors huddled under a bush, which presented a far greater risk of freezin'."

Skye made a distressed sound, then quickly dipped her chin and studied her porridge with admirable concentration.

Quinn barely suppressed a triumphant grin.

*She cares.*

Delight soared through him, sending a joyful symphony tunneling through his veins. "Benedict wouldna have thanked me for the latter either." He skewed his mouth sideways, a trifle self-consciously. "He's a wee bit spoiled. Likes his comfort, he does."

"As do we all," the dowager baroness murmured distractedly while giving Skye a perceptive glance. Not much escaped Liam's mother's hawk-like attention. Her focus shifted to Quinn, her keen gaze drilling into his soul. "Please, fill yer plate and join us."

After a moment, Skye drew her gaze upward. "How is your horse?"

"Verra well. His leg has been tended to, and he's warm and comfortable in the stables." Quinn ambled to the sideboard and, after helping himself to a generous amount of food, considered the three empty seats. Without a hint a of reservation, he placed his plate in front of the chair beside Skye, fully aware his action spoke volumes to all present.

*Fine.*

Quinn wanted them all to know what he harbored in his lost and lonely soul.

He pointedly disregarded Liam's dark eyebrows elevating an inch as he veered his gaze just as meaningfully at another chair.

*Sorry, old chap.*

"Ye entered through the kitchen?" Emeline asked, sending her husband a half-bewildered, half-concerned look. "Shouldna the doors be locked at night against vagabonds and the like?"

Sinking onto his seat and snapping his serviette open, Quinn wagged his eyebrows. "Who said they werena, my lady?"

Kendra giggled, and Skye's rosy lips swept upward too.

Her ladyship's eyes rounded. Clearly uncertain

70

how to respond, she cut Liam a glance, but with the aplomb of a princess, she wrested her surprise under control. "Quinn, ye ken we dinna stand on ceremony. Please call me Emeline."

"How many times have I asked ye no' to pick the locks?" Liam resumed his seat and leveled him a reproachful stare.

Quinn hitched a shoulder as he cut into his sausage. "I was tryin' to be considerate and no' wake yer household at the ungodly hour. I'm sure yer housekeeper and butler are grateful for my thoughtfulness, even if ye are no'."

Liam made a rude noise under his breath.

"Aye, so sneakin' into our house in the middle of the night is considerate?" Arms folded, Kendra teased, mock annoyance in her tone. "What if ye'd disturbed a servant or Liam and found yerself shot as a result? I think that would've been quite inconsiderate. I really canna tolerate the sight of blood."

Eyebrow cocked, Quinn stabbed his sausage with his fork. "Och, lass. I'm always verra, verra careful."

"You make a habit of picking locks?" Skye asked,

a degree of disquiet in her amused eyes. "It makes me rather wonder why the skill is necessary."

"I'll tell ye all about that business later," he said with a brazen wink.

And he would. There'd be no secrets between them. She'd know about his father and grandfather and his intentions to continue aiding those subjected to enslavement in any form.

"As always, 'tis good to see ye again, Quinn." Picking up her fork once more, the dowager baroness curved her mouth and angled her head toward Skye. "What do ye think about a Christmas celebration? Have ye ever observed the occasion?"

"Me? Nae, no' that I can recall." He rubbed the bridge of his nose. "Mayhap as a wee bairn. My mother was English, ye ken, but I think it a marvelous notion." He bent slightly nearer Skye, murmuring for her ears alone, "I'm most happy to see ye in good spirits, Miss Hendron."

Her color remained high, and she fidgeted with her serviette. She swept a quick glance around the table before speaking low. "You were gone so long. I'd begun to despair that you would ever return."

"I vowed I would. Nothin' but death itself could keep me away, *leannan*."

"Oh." At the whispered endearment, a pleased flush brought another rush of pink to her cheeks. "Did everything go as you'd hoped?"

"Indeed." Reaching for his coffee, he lowered his chin. "I had some loose ends to tie up. Now, however, I'm my own man and free to do what I please. Do tell me about this fête ye're plannin'."

Beaming from ear to ear, Kendra piped up. "Skye wants to have a Christmastide celebration at Eytone Hall. I've heard tell of such marvelous things the English and others do to commemorate the occasion."

"I think 'tis a wonderful idea too." Enthusiasm sparkled in Emeline's eyes. "And I dinna think we should make it a quiet affair either. As ye said, Liam, though the Kirk might frown on some of the more pagan traditions, there's nae law forbiddin' us from hostin' a house party where we just *happen* to offer a few Christmas traditions as entertainment."

"Have I married myself a rebel?" Liam asked with

an affectionate grin.

She laid her fingertips atop the back of his hand. "Liam, why dinna we invite the Kennedys and the Wallaces?"

"I think ye'd need to invite the Rutherfords and the McGregors as well," Liam advised. "All live within easy travelin' distance, and I believe they'd enjoy the gatherin' as much as us."

Kendra made a disgruntled noise, her fine raven eyebrows swooping low in consternation. "Must we invite *all* of the McGregors?"

"Yes. We must." Her mother speared her a quelling look. "Ye ken Broden is like kin to us."

"No' all of us," Kendra muttered, her expression sour. "He's a giant pain in the arse to some. A great, nasty, puss-laden carbuncle on the bum."

"Kendra Eislyn Olive MacKay, watch yer language," the dowager baroness reproached. "If we're invitin' the others, we must invite the Duke of Roxdale, his wards, and yer cousin, Bryston McPherson."

Would Skye mind all of the extra people she

wasn't acquainted with?

She was in mourning, after all.

Had she wanted an intimate gathering, and now the whole affair was expanding into something vastly different? Her eagerness had kindled a good deal more zeal in the MacKays than Quinn would've expected.

She didn't appear the least disgruntled, however. As a matter of fact, he'd never seen her so animated. Mayhap, she enjoyed entertaining. A drifter himself, the closest thing he'd ever come to hosting anything was inviting a chap to share an ale or a finger's worth of whisky at a pub.

After she agreed to marry him, they'd have to discuss where she wanted to live. He had no preference where he put down roots, but he expected she'd want to be near her only remaining family.

Inhaling a bracing breath, he took another step toward propriety. "If it wouldna be an imposition, might my grandmother be invited? I am the only family she has left."

## 8

"**O**f course, she should come," Skye agreed at once. "I would very much enjoy meeting her."

"I didna ken ye had any family," Liam observed, his probing stare attempting to peel away the layers of subterfuge Quinn had hidden behind for so long. "I'd like to make her acquaintance as well."

"I should warn ye," Quinn said, recalling the oversized purple wig complete with a miniature ship she'd been wearing when he'd called upon her. "She's outspoken and more than a bit eccentric. I believe, at last count, she had nine cats—named after one mythological goddess or another—and they each have a place set for them to dine each mornin' and evenin'. I believe it would do her a world of good to socialize."

Maybe she'd stop treating the furballs like pampered children if she spent more time with humans.

"She sounds delightful." Skye took a dainty bite of what now must be cold porridge. "Is she your maternal or paternal grandmother?"

"Maternal. A dotty but dear thing." Oddly, the usual ire Quinn experienced whenever his thoughts took him down the unpleasant path to his paternity didn't burgeon within him. Mayhap, he could put the ugliness that had haunted his soul to rest at last.

The dowager baroness nodded, her face contemplative. "Aye, I like the idea. What we do in the privacy of our home is our business. And as Liam said, 'tis no' illegal to celebrate Christmas. Emeline, ye are mistress of this house. What are yer thoughts?"

Emeline sent Skye an encouraging smile. "Why dinna we meet in the rose salon this afternoon at three of the clock and discuss our thoughts and ideas?" She gravitated her gaze to the dowager baroness and Kendra to include them as well.

Afternoon was perfect.

Quinn intended to request a meeting with Liam to ask for Skye's hand in marriage, and then he'd invite Skye for a stroll later this morning and ask her to marry him. He cut Liam a side-eyed look and couldn't help but chuckle at his wry, befuddled expression. "It seems, my friend, the ladies have this under control."

"'Tis a good thing too, because beyond a Christmas goose and a yule log, I havena the first idea what is called for. A right good scotch or cognac, I suppose. I dinna recall Christmastide ever bein' celebrated in this house." A hoary, grayish snout appeared over the table's edge, snuffling loudly and clearly seeking a treat.

Liam obliged with half a scone, and the snout disappeared only to be followed by loud chomping.

"Do stop feedin' him at the table, Liam. His manners are already atrocious," his mother admonished, shaking her head. "As for Christmastide, it hasna been observed here. But that disna mean we canna start new traditions."

"Precisely," Emeline said, one finger on her chin and eyes slightly narrowed. "I'll speak with the cook today. I have several ideas for festive foods. Black bun, for one." She clasped her hands. "We simply must have black bun and clootie dumplin', of course."

With each passing minute, Quinn appreciated the idea of Christmas festivities more and more. By God, when was the last time he'd eaten black bun? His mouth practically watered in anticipation.

"Oh, and wassail and mulled cider," Skye put in. "And ginger biscuits and iced gingerbread."

"And mince pies?" Kendra asked hopefully. "Sugar plums?"

Quinn couldn't abide mince pie, and from the tiny twitch of Skye's nose, he'd wager she bore no fondness for the novelty either. Mayhap that's why Cromwell had pies outlawed for several years too. Sugar plums, however, were another matter entirely.

"We'll all be fat as hogs by Hogmanay." Humor pleated the corners of Liam's eyes belying any real censure. With an almost boyish grin, he said, "I quite favor marzipan, myself."

"Then, of course, we shall add it to the menu." Skye laughed and shook her head, dislodging a soft, honey-colored curl. It slid to her temple to join the other tendrils framing her face.

Quinn balled his hand to keep from tucking the strand behind her ear.

"I fear my small celebration is going to become quite an event." She gave everyone a winsome smile. "But the merriment is meant to be shared, is it not?"

"I believe our friends will be as delighted at the novelty as we are, my dear." The dowager baroness bestowed a doting smile on her niece.

Beneath the cover of the tablecloth, Quinn gathered Skye's hand into his own.

He barely bit back a chuckle at all of the activity going on beneath the tablecloth.

For an instant, she stiffened before her fingers curled around his.

She didn't glance in his direction, but a rosy flush swept up her porcelain cheeks. His heart swelled with happiness to see the color in her face, a smile curving her pretty mouth, and cheer twinkling in her eyes once more. She'd been sad for almost as long as he'd known her.

"I know mistletoe is rare in the Highlands, and I don't expect we'll be able to do much in the way of decorating with greenery." Skye turned her attention to the garden beyond the other window. "But I imagine there's enough rosemary and other plants of one sort or another to make a kissing bough."

Quinn quite liked the sound of that.

Beneath the table, she gave his fingers a suggestive squeeze.

Why, the darling lass flirted with him.

He squeezed back, and she bit her lip.

Liam shook his head. "No' a bit of it, Skye. Quinn and I and a few of the tenants can journey to the Lowlands. We can collect greeneries and perhaps the mistletoe as well. Holly and pine are also plentiful there." Even he seemed excited about the festivities.

Emeline, her face alight with enthusiasm, tapped the table with her fingertips. "Aye, we'll have to purchase supplies anyway, so that's a perfect opportunity. Och, we should have dancin' too, I think."

A shadow flitted across Skye's face. "I'm not sure how much dancing I should do. I'm still in mourning, after all. I didn't mean for this to become a production. I don't want to inconvenience the staff or cause them more work."

Liam's wife waved a graceful hand. "Nonsense, Skye. I for one am verra curious about Christmas traditions. My aunt didna observe the holiday at all, and a little dancin' would do ye good, I think. Besides, ye'll be with family and friends and nae one is goin' to scowl at ye for enjoyin' yerself."

Liam had found himself a rare gem in Emeline MacKay.

Eyes shiny, Kendra leaned forward. "Are we goin' to exchange gifts?"

Quinn glanced around the table.

He already had a gift for Skye. He'd purchased the Luckenbooth brooch in Edinburgh, meaning to give it to her for a betrothal present. It would suit just as well as a Christmas gift and if all went well with Liam today, the brooch would also mark their upcoming nuptials.

"I think that's acceptable. Nothin' expensive, just tokens. After all, the season isna about gifts." Liam leveled him a hard, piercing look, which Quinn responded to with a glib smile.

"I dinna ken about that. The Magi brought gifts to the baby Jesus," Quinn unnecessarily reminded Liam. "Verra valuable gifts for that time period, if I recall my history correctly."

He wasn't going to allow Liam's cantankerous glowers, grimaces, or scowls to discourage him. God's teeth, he hadn't humbled himself, accepted his inheritance, and resigned his position for a cause he believed in with every fiber of his being to allow Liam to deny him the thing that he most wanted in the world.

"I believe 'tis customary to give a token to the staff as well," Liam's mother murmured, a slight crease between her brows. "Though I have nae idea what would be appropriate."

"Mama and Papa always gave them coin since the servants knew best what they were most in need of." Skye waved her free hand. "And usually a couple boxes of bonbons or other sweets. They were permitted a special feast of their own and dancing belowstairs as well."

Quinn ran his thumb across the back of Skye's hand and felt her tremble. This extraordinary woman was worth every sacrifice he'd made, and every one he'd make for years to come. She cut him a sidelong glance, her sweet mouth sweeping upward, and he knew beyond any doubt that he'd made the right choice.

He'd chosen her.

Liam stood, and Prince lumbered to his side. "Ladies, if ye'll excuse me. I've much work to do. Especially if I'm to take a few days to fetch supplies and greeneries for ye." He directed his attention to Quinn. "When ye're finished with yer meal, please come to my office. I've a few things to discuss with ye."

His fork at his mouth, Quinn paused, glancing upward.

*I'll just bet ye do.*

Liam wore an indiscernible expression, and that proved worrisome given the inflection Quinn had detected in his voice.

Skye glanced between the two of them, a tiny,

troubled furrow between her winged blonde eyebrows. Ah, she'd heard the nuance in his tone too.

"Of course. I shouldna be more than a quarter of an hour." With deliberate nonchalance, Quinn turned his attention back to his eggs. Best to not let Liam see he had any concerns. He'd not be dissuaded in his quest. Skye would be his, and he'd prefer to remain Liam's friend afterward.

Feeling Liam's intense gaze on him, he looked up and forced a genial smile.

With a rather brusque nod, and his mother watching his retreat with a speculative glance, Liam quit the room.

"Ye've been well?" Quinn asked Skye in a low tone meant for her ears only. "And Patches?"

Skye brushed an orange cat hair from her sleeve. "Yes, we are both fine," she responded just as quietly. "She continues to give Aunt Louisa fits though."

"Skye?" Aunt Louisa said, drawing her attention. "Would it be appropriate to hire a string quartet?"

Quinn would wager Benedict she'd noticed the private exchange between him and Skye, and this was her way of bringing it to an end. It did rather gall to be such a close family friend and yet still be considered so utterly unbefitting to be Skye's suitor or husband.

"I think that is a fantastic suggestion." Skye's swift sideways glance and the tiny upward tilt of her lips revealed she'd guessed her aunt's true motive too.

"Which day would we have dancin'?" Dowager Baroness Penderhaven asked. "I believe there are twelve days of revelry, are there no'?"

"Yes, we always had guests and a grand feast the evening of Christmas Day. Other activities and entertainments were planned over the course of the other days, with the festivities culminating on January fifth." Sadness transformed her countenance for a minute. No doubt, planning the merriment was bittersweet for her.

"Well, we mightna be able to celebrate as masterfully as my sister did every year but I, for one, think 'tis a marvelous way to commemorate Martha's and Charles's memories." The dowager baroness's eyes grew misty, and she blinked rapidly. "I'm so glad ye suggested it Skye. I think it may be just what we all needed."

Quinn bent near, whispering in Skye's ear. "Just

seein' ye again is all I need to make this the most marvelous Christmas ever."

Such a ridiculous thing to say. He'd already admitted to never having participated in holiday jollity before. Still, he meant the sentiment behind his words.

Her eyes softened, and he had to set his jaw to keep from sweeping her into his arms and tasting her mouth. When her focus trailed to his lips, he knew beyond a doubt she harbored thoughts of kissing him too, and he stifled a groan.

She cleared her throat and averted her gaze. "Do you have any special dishes you'd like prepared for Twelfth Night, Quinn?"

A long-ago, hazy memory stirred of his mother placing a serving of orange pudding before him. He'd always adored the dessert but, until this moment, had forgotten the first time he'd tasted the delicious treat.

"Orange puddin'." The words slipped from his mouth before he realized it. "My mother used to make it."

"Mine did too," she whispered.

"Walk with me, Skye," Quinn said impulsively. He needed to see her alone, away from curious eyes and ears, so he could tell her unfettered what brewed in his heart. "Tis cold, but if we bundle ourselves, it shouldna be too uncomfortable."

"All right." Her attention scooted to one of the windows and the sun streaming through the melting frost on the pane. "It's really quite lovely outdoors with frost covering everything."

Most women would've refused him outright, so cold was it outside. He hoped that meant she was as eager to be alone with him as he was with her.

Painfully aware three pairs of eyes regarded them with acute interest, he said, "I'll see what Liam needs to speak with me about, and I'll meet ye in the rose salon in an hour. Will that be convenient for ye?"

As if she'd suddenly become aware of those peering at them, Skye withdrew her hand from his and angled her head. "Yes, that's fine."

After excusing himself, Quinn made straight for Liam's study. If Liam refused his request for her hand, would Skye consider eloping? Would her family disown her if he did? Ballocks, he couldn't ask that of her.

Mouth pressed into a grim line, he strode the corridor to Liam's study, very real anxiety knotting his stomach.

## 9

As promised, an hour later, bundled in so many clothes and outerwear she could scarcely move her arms, Skye awaited Quinn in the rather gaudy rose salon. Arm in arm, Emeline and Kendra had gone off toward the ballroom, their heads bent near. Probably already making holiday plans.

Aunt Louisa sat before the robust fire knitting.

Patches had been banned to the kitchen after a well-executed sneak attack on an unsuspecting skein and hopelessly tangling the wool.

Skye was quite sure she sweated like a lathered racehorse beneath her many layers of clothing, and if Quinn didn't arrive soon, she'd be forced to start peeling clothing from her person.

"I really should insist someone chaperone ye, but I

wouldna force anyone into the frigid weather." Aunt Louisa glanced up from whatever the black thing was she knitted. "I shall ask ye to stroll along the terrace, so I can see ye from the window."

Located on the rear side of the house, the terrace enjoyed afternoon sun when there was any to be had. As the clock had not yet chimed ten, deep shadows covered the flagstone, and the frost hadn't begun to thaw there.

Skye had rather hoped to walk in a sunnier location, but she'd not argue the point for fear a chaperone would be procured, and then any opportunity to converse privately with Quinn would be lost.

"Of course, Aunt Louisa."

Her aunt must know she wouldn't do anything improper, but now that Liam was her guardian, she supposed they must take a more active interest in Skye's activities and whom she entertained.

Earlier, when Quinn had entered the breakfast room, her heart had fluttered like a wild bird in her breast. Such giddiness had sluiced through her that her doldrums of the night before seemed trite and nonsensical. The promise in his warm, green gaze when it had rested upon her had given her great hope.

Careful not to appear too eager, Skye slid a sidelong glance to the still empty doorframe, then to the mantel clock. Quinn was six minutes late but, likely, he'd left his overcoat in his bedchamber which was in the manor's other wing.

Even as she finished the thought, he strode through the doorway with animalistic ease and grace, holding his black cocked hat. That charming smile, which never failed to make her stomach do strange things, quirked his mouth. Lord but he was striking. If she lived to be a toothless, gray-haired, old tabby, he'd never fail to stir her this way.

"Please forgive my tardiness." He didn't offer an explanation but canted his head toward the Dowager Baroness Penderhaven as he extended his elbow to Skye. "Are ye ready?"

"Yes." She gathered her muff and placed her hand in the bend of his elbow.

"Quinn, I already advised Skye, and I'll request

the same from ye. Make yer stroll up and down the terrace so that I can see ye. It wouldna do to raise eyebrows or create gossip fodder."

"As ye will, my lady," he intoned quite formally with a slight tilt of his head as he placed his hat atop his light brown hair.

Skye prudently refrained from reminding her aunt that she'd walked alone with him dozens of times before he'd departed. No doubt, Aunt Louisa had noted Quinn's marked interest in her at breakfast—as had Liam—and decided to take her duties as chaperone more judiciously.

Neither Skye nor Quinn spoke as he escorted her to the entrance, and Simmons opened the double doors for them. The sun had melted the morning frost on this side of the house, but Quinn was still careful as he guided her down the steps, lest she slip.

They circled the manor and, as directed, stepped onto the terrace and proceeded to wander its length. Wiggling his gloved fingers in a cocky manner, he winked at the dowager baroness as they passed the window.

Skye smothered the giggle rising to her throat at his antics, not at all certain in her current mood that Aunt Louisa would appreciate her mirth.

Her aunt gave him a somber nod before returning her attention back to her knitting. Skye hadn't missed the corners of her aunt's mouth twitching at his silliness.

Only he could take a severe situation and, with a dab of mirth, lighten the mood.

Tucking her palm more firmly into his elbow, Quinn placed his other hand atop hers. "I missed ye, Skye."

She'd already learned he wasn't a man prone to flowery phrases or poetic nonsense, despite his witticisms. He said what he thought and what was in his heart.

"I missed you, too. Very much." So very much she feared her heart would truly break when he hadn't returned when he said he would.

They'd reached the far end of the pavers, and she gasped, pointing to a frost-covered cobweb spun between a nearby shrub's bare branches. "Oh, Quinn, look. It's as delicate as spun lace. Isn't it beautiful?"

"'Tis, indeed." He smiled down into her upturned face, grazing a fingertip over her cheek. "Ye are far more exquisite."

She permitted her eyelids to flutter closed, and a contented sigh whispered past her parted lips. She was certain he meant to kiss her.

"We'd best keep walkin' else the dowager baroness will come lookin' for us, love," he murmured in his soft brogue.

That was another thing she adored about him. When he spoke, she could listen forever to the musical lilt of his deep voice. She opened her eyes to find dual green pools gazing at her longingly. Swallowing and wresting her desire under control, she yanked her gaze away.

They took up their stroll again, but they'd only gone a few paces before Skye chuckled. "I don't understand the sudden need for all this propriety. We've been alone many times before, and neither Liam nor Aunt Louisa was the least concerned. Why the sudden change?"

"Och, well, they're nae numpty fools." He cast a quick downward glance to meet her eyes before staring straight ahead once more. "They ken that I have the highest regard for ye."

*Regard?*

That was a far cry from love; at least to her way of thinking.

Gaze lowered, she idly noted the soft crunching sound their feet made on the frosty flagstone. She had the highest regard for several men, none of whom made her breath hitch in her lungs, her heart beat with the cadence of a hundred African drums, or who made her feel wholly complete, as if her soul had found its other half.

Disappointment reared its pointy little head and proceeded to mockingly poke her with its sharp talons.

Had she misunderstood Quinn?

His happiness at seeing her again?

Surely not. He'd held her hand beneath the table, risking Liam's wrath if caught.

But...he had been slightly reserved and lost in thought since entering the parlor. Just what had transpired between him and Liam?

They passed the salon windows, but neither glanced toward the house this time. She was afraid Aunt Louisa would read the frustration and pique on her countenance and mistake its cause. She hoped her bonnet's brim hid her face sufficiently not to raise concern.

Skye brought her gaze up to meet Quinn's pale green eyes. Gentleness and warmth glinted in their depths, yet a flintiness hardened his jaw that hadn't been there at breakfast.

"Skye…?"

Drawing her to a stop next to a quaint wrought iron bench, he shifted his attention to the frost-laden lawns. This reticent man before her had replaced the charming, carefree rogue from breakfast. The air was surprisingly still and quiet, and if her nerves hadn't been rattled by his change in demeanor, she would've savored the peace.

Instead, she studied the planes and angles of his face, the flexing muscles, the air of bleakness about him. Whatever he wanted to say, it wasn't a marriage proposal. Dying a little inside, she forced her lips upward at the corners.

"Yes?" My, she sounded composed and not the least befuddled.

"I asked Liam for yer hand in marriage." His mouth pulled into a taut ribbon, he gathered one of her hands in his. He didn't act like a man who'd had his request granted. A man facing the gallows showed more cheer.

"What did he say?" Fearing she already knew the answer, she swallowed the sudden constriction in her throat.

*How could Liam? How could he?*

And what was more, why?

Why had he refused Quinn?

She knew why, the wretched addlepate.

*I'll never forgive him. I shan't.*

Because, even though Quinn was his close friend and welcome in his home, Liam considered him an irresponsible libertine.

Quinn wasn't good enough for her.

*But he is. He is perfect for me.*

How dare Liam?

He'd only been her guardian for two months, and he thought he had the right to make such a life-altering decision for her? Without even discussing Quinn's proposal with her? Didn't she have any say in the matter?

She dragged in a juddery breath, putting a halt to her wildly cavorting thoughts. She must give Quinn time to explain before stirring herself into a froth.

He laced the fingers of his hand with hers, a wry smile playing about the edges of his mouth. The humor didn't soften the rest of his features. "He dinna say aye, but I'm no' ready to quit the field just yet."

Determination emphasized the last few words.

What, precisely, had Liam said then?

All her earlier cheer about the prospect of planning a Christmas celebration flew away on the whisper of a breeze that gently flicked her bonnet's ribbons. She bit the inside of her cheek to smother a very unladylike retort about her cousin.

Quinn lifted her fingers to his mouth, pressing a kiss to her knuckles. "Tell me I'm no' mistaken, and ye return my affection? Because I vowed to him, and I shall to ye as well, if that is the case, I willna give up. Ever. I shall prove myself to him and ye and the whole world if I must."

A tremulous smile bending her lips, Skye touched his cheek. "Oh, Quinn. I do return your affections. I...I love you, and I thought my heart broken when you didn't return as you'd promised. I could see no future, no happiness, without you."

Green fire sparked in his irises, and he dared edge nearer, until his thighs touched her cloak. "Skye, love, I am humbled and thrilled to hear those words from yer pretty lips. I love ye, my bonnie English lass. And I promise, somehow, we'll be together. I've only to convince Liam that I can be a good husband to ye. That I can love and honor ye in the manner ye deserve."

His sweet words caused her eyes to grow misty.

How she loved this man.

"We'd better continue our stroll," he suggested with a side-eyed glance.

They resumed walking, lest Aunt Louisa send a

servant in search of them.

"Why would Liam think otherwise?" she asked.

They'd reached the end of the terrace once more and turned to retrace their steps. Again, when they passed the salon window, he made a point of giving the dowager baroness a cheeky wave.

Chuckling, she shook her head.

"You are incorrigible, Quinn," Skye admonished with a giggle. "Shouldn't you be on your best behavior to win Aunt Louisa's and Liam's approval?"

Pointing his attention overhead, his countenance grew solemn once more. "Though I dinna consider myself to be a wicked man, Skye, I've no' been a saint either. Liam kens this above all others. But he also kens how loyal and steadfast I am. And I'm countin' on that to win him over. I confess, I admire him for protectin' ye, even if it exasperates me."

"We can convince him together," she said. The Christmas house party might prove to be the perfect opportunity to do just that. "I'll tell him I'll have no other, and I know he won't condemn me to a life of spinsterhood."

At least she didn't think he would.

Emeline and Kendra wouldn't let him.

Neither, she strongly suspected, would Aunt Louisa. By no means was Skye a pampered, cossetted miss accustomed to having her own way. Even though an only child, her parents had taken great pains to ensure she wasn't spoiled. However, in this instance, she would remain adamant.

She would be Quinn's wife.

"I want ye to ken that I have my own fortune, Skye. That was one of the reasons I had to leave. I've been estranged from my family for some time, but I kent that to make ye my bride, I needed to set my affairs in order and accept my inheritance."

"I'll take you just the way you are, Quinn. That's the man I fell in love with. You needn't change anything for me."

"I want to." His arm tensed beneath her fingers, and she realized he spoke the truth. "Liam was surprised when I informed him that I possess my own wealth. He admitted to suspectin' I might've had my eyes on yer inheritance." Another rueful grin quirked his mouth. "If I wasna tryin' to win his approval, I would've clocked him for the insult."

Skye looked askance at him, all outraged, kittenish fury.

"I never for an instant considered you might be a fortune hunter." She wrinkled her nose in remembered distaste. "I've been the unfortunate target of several previously—four, to be exact—and I assure you, I know precisely what to look for. I'm surprised you're not more offended that Liam would accuse you of such a dishonorable thing."

He canted his head and hitched a shoulder. "He has reason to doubt me."

She started to protest, but he held up his hand.

"Hear me out. I'll have nae secrets between us. Ye must ken exactly the kind of man ye are agreein' to spend the rest of yer life with."

Examining his serious expression, she was half-afraid to hear what he wanted to tell her. Nevertheless, she dipped her chin. "Please, go on."

"For the past decade, I've worked with a covert group to help no' only West African slaves, but also children and adults forced into servitude and indentured service." Scorn and wrath laced his snipped words.

Skye flinched, having never seen him angry before. He obviously had very strong feelings about these issues.

"I resigned my position because a married man needs to care for his wife and family foremost." His sideways smile appeared almost apologetic. "It wouldna be honorable of me to take ye to wife, and then risk my life kennin' ye'd be left alone. Especially if there are wee bairns."

A lovely feeling fluttered in her belly because he'd make such a sacrifice for her. And because the idea of bearing his children thrilled mightily. It also humbled her and made her all that much more certain of his noble character.

"But," he continued, "even though slavery and indentured service is legal, ye should ken that I shall continue to fight those atrocities in other ways." A fierceness entered his voice and turned his visage stony. "I can never accept men enslavin' their fellow man."

Her eyes blurry from unshed tears, Skye nodded vigorously.

"I agree, Quinn. Slavery is awful. One time when I was in London with Mama and Papa, we saw people with their hands tied being dragged onto a ship against their wills." Tears ran down her cheeks. "There were small children crying and begging for their parents. I don't understand how people can treat others like that."

Quinn fished a handkerchief from his pocket and passed it to her.

After blotting her eyes and cheeks, she returned it to him. "Thank you. I didn't think to bring a hankie out with me."

"There are people who are good and decent and honorable to their verra core, and there are others who are rotten and foul to the marrow." He scowled, brushing a gloved hand over his eyes as if unbearably weary or to erase a memory. "My father and grandfather were the latter. Ye should ken, they participated in the enslavement of innocent people. That's why I was estranged from them, and why I refused my inheritance."

She clasped a hand to her mouth, staring at him in horror and sympathy. "Oh, Quinn. I'm so sorry. How that must haunt you."

"It did for a verra long time." His expression grew intense, and he trailed his gaze over her face. "Until I met ye. Now though, *leannan,* I believe I can put that behind me, and I can use my monies to help others." Mirth crinkled his eyes as he flicked the tip of her cold nose. "Isna that what Christmas is truly about? Carin' for our fellow man?"

"It is, indeed." Skye hadn't a doubt that her eyes shone with admiration and love. "What shall we do about Liam?"

A genuine smile wreathed his face. "My darlin' bonnie lass, even though Liam has initially said nae, I believe he will eventually say aye. How can he stand in the way of true love?"

"He must agree, for as I said, I shall have no other," Skye vowed.

It was most unfortunate that Liam had control of her inheritance until she turned one and twenty. But she'd read her father's will, and her bequeathment could not be withheld from her after that. For any reason.

Growing serious once more, Quinn urged her around the house's corner. After looking in both directions, he enfolded her in his arms, and a delicious thrill zipped to her toes. He cupped her face with one hand, emotion darkening his eyes to a riveting jade.

"Though I canna officially request yer hand, Skye, I humbly ask ye to consider becomin' my wife."

"Yes, Quinn. Yes. Yes." The icy ache in her heart was thawing. Because of this brave, strong and wonderfully unique man, she could feel happiness and joy again. "Yes, Quinn. I'll marry you and, together, we'll convince Liam that it is the best thing for both of us."

"And if he still refuses?" He lowered his head until his lips were but an inch from hers.

Lifting onto her toes, she braced her hands on his shoulders, whispering, "We'll cross that bridge when we come to it."

Then his lips were on hers, taking her mouth in a searing kiss that made her forget all else.

## 10

The next fortnight was a whirlwind of activity. Invitations were sent out and accepted by all. Supplies were ordered, and instead of leaving to gather the various greeneries required to decorate Eytone Hall, Liam had requested that the Duke of Roxdale bring them with him.

The duke and his wards, Bethea and Branwen Glanville, had been the last to arrive two days ago with an entire wagon filled with various greens. Since then, amidst laughter and animated conversation, as well as copious amounts of tea, coffee, brandy, and various dainties, everyone had been about one task or another helping with the preparations.

With the help of Marjorie Kennedy, also an Englishwoman, Skye had delegated various responsibilities to others.

An air of anticipation and giddiness permeated Eytone Hall, and she smiled to herself more than once at the almost childish anticipation of the guests and her family. Quinn, too, seemed caught up in the spirit, although she'd come upon him deep in thought multiple times.

He'd smile and, after a hasty glance around, would pull her into a corner or a corridor for a very satisfying kiss. Or two. Or five. Each day, she fell impossibly more in love with him. Not marrying him didn't bear contemplating.

They would wed. Somehow. Someway.

The Christmas ball was the day after tomorrow, and she hummed to herself as she finished tying a gold ribbon around the last gift she'd wrapped. Her trip to the village last week had proved quite satisfactory.

She'd purchased an elaborate lace fichu for Aunt Louisa, a pair of evening gloves embroidered with silver and gold thread for Kendra, and a delicate pink crocheted shawl for Emeline. A silver-plated inkwell set had been selected for Liam and, after much thought, she'd settled on a gold pocket watch for Quinn.

At her behest, the jeweler etched the image of a bird in flight on the inside of the case. It was the only thing she could think of that represented freedom for all. She'd been tempted to also have the jeweler etch an endearment, but she suspected Liam might want to exclaim over the gift as people were wont to do.

An etching could be added later.

She continued humming as she gathered the packages and left her chamber, heading for the formal drawing room. That was where Emeline and Aunt Louisa had decided to conduct most of the Twelfth Night activities.

The room had been transformed into a cheerful array of holly and pine boughs, sprigs of rosemary, ivy, and numerous bows. Many of the other rooms were similarly decorated, giving the mansion a splendid holiday atmosphere.

Two additional footmen and three maids had been hired from the village to assist with their guests' needs, as well as the revelry preparations.

As she descended the stairs, Arieen Wallace, Mayra Rutherford, and Berget Kennedy tumbled into the entry, holding their stomachs and swiping at their eyes, amid gales of laughter.

Upon spying Skye, Mayra smiled and waved her forward. "Come, Skye, join us. Emeline and Kendra are insistin' we participate in a skit. The men are tasked with doin' so as well." She snickered and grinned widely. "They're practicin' right now."

"Not willingly." Arieen disagreed with a slight shake of her raven head, amusement fairly dancing in her green eyes. "They're arguing and strutting about."

Skye couldn't imagine any of the brawny Highlanders willingly doing so.

Berget glanced over her shoulder and erupted into another fit of giggles. "Aye, they're supposed to be the shepherds that the angels appeared to. I can't wait to hear what they think the shepherds might've been saying or doing."

Nor, truth be told, could Skye.

Mayra puffed out her chest and lowered her chin, saying in a deep, gravelly voice, "Ye great clod head, did ye give us tainted whisky? I vow I see men wearin' women's gowns and floatin' about singin' gibberish."

"Can you imagine what they think the heavenly hosts will say?" Arieen quipped between giggles. "Bryston McPherson and Camden Kennedy both threatened to go home when they were assigned the roles of lambs."

A new chorus of laughter filled the entryway, and Skye joined in their merriment.

She was only too glad to leave the chore of organizing the entertainment to Emeline and Kendra. What she thought would be a small family gathering had blossomed into something much more, and though she didn't mind the extra work, she appreciated all the help she could muster.

She glanced from woman to woman expectantly. "So, what's our skit to be about it?"

"We're performin' Jesus's birth, except it will be told from the perspective of the animals in the manger."

Lips twitching, Skye raised an eyebrow. "Both of these skits smack of Kendra's sense of humor."

"Aye," Berget agreed as she fell in step with Arianne behind Mayra and Skye. "She has a wicked wit. She also vowed that anyone who didn't participate wouldn't be allowed any of the delicious confections being prepared in the kitchens."

Ah, and now Skye knew precisely why the men had conceded. She'd seen that lot eat. Very sly of Kendra, and she couldn't help but admire her cousin's cunning and initiative.

"Please, give me a moment to leave these gifts in the drawing room." With a small upward bend of her mouth, she slipped into the room and placed the gifts on the appointed table. A few others had already been left there as well. Catching her lower lip between her teeth, a slight feeling of misgiving swept her.

Perhaps she should've considered giving gifts to the other women as well, but wouldn't that have made them feel obligated in turn? In addition to Berget, Arieen, and Mayra, Marjorie Kennedy and her two darling little red-haired girls, as well as Bethea and Branwen Glanville—the Duke of Roxdale's wards—were here.

Giving a slight shake of her head, she turned away from the table.

This gathering wasn't about exchanging gifts. It was about spending time with family and friends. The merest hint of sadness shrouded her for a moment when she again recalled that this would be her first Christmas without her parents.

Yes, but it would also be her first Christmas—God willing, of many—with Quinn. That knowledge quite put her in a cheerful mood. With each passing day—no hour—she grew to love him more. And if Liam remained obstinate and uncompromising, she would elope with Quinn.

Love like theirs was too precious and rare to cast aside.

She joined the other ladies in the corridor, and they made their way to the solarium to practice their skit.

Three hours later, she escaped with the excuse she needed to speak with Eytone Hall's cook. Still chuckling under her breath at the silliness she'd been partaking in, she shook her head. Not only had Kendra and Emeline assigned each of the women the role of various animals—Skye was an Egyptian camel—the beasts had accents.

Horrible, hysterical accents.

A French cow. A Swiss goat. A Spanish donkey. A German lamb. An Italian ox...

If nothing else, they would all laugh.

She had just enough time to check with Mrs. Spence to make sure all the food preparations were coming along before she must change for dinner and the charades afterward. Charades—another one of Kendra's ideas, complete with a Christmastide theme.

So far, everyone had good-naturedly participated in the activities with patience and good cheer. Not for the want of a few rolled eyes and grumbles beneath the gentlemen's breaths.

A grin tipped her lips upward.

Knowing Kendra's penchant for outrageousness, someone might very well be pretending to bray like a donkey or ride a camel tonight. She just hoped it wasn't her. A throaty chuckle escaped her. Watching Quinn do either might prove highly amusing, however.

As Skye turned the corner to descend into the kitchen, a man's arm snaked around her waist.

A startled squeak caught in her throat, and she twisted this way and that to see who'd snared her. Although, she already had a pretty good idea who the villain might be. Quinn's unique outdoorsy, spicy scent wafted around her, and she relaxed into his strong embrace.

"Quinn," she chided. "We're going to be caught."

"Shh, my love. I havena had a moment alone with ye in two days. When Liam hasna had me at one task or another—I vow to keep me from ye—Grandmother has demanded my attention." Quinn pressed a kiss to her forehead. "And I dinna care if we are outed. Then yer stubborn cousin would be marchin' us before the cleric in a trice."

Yes, but at what cost?

Besides, Quinn was too much of a gentleman to ruin her to gain what he wanted. He'd never use such nefarious means to win her hand. Even if she wouldn't mind it too awfully much if he did. Skye had learned one very surprising thing about herself this past fortnight.

A wanton streak ran through her.

At least when it came to Quinn's kisses and caresses.

Slipping her arms around his waist, she stepped nearer, savoring the feeling of his arms encircling her and the wide expanse of his hard chest pressing against her breasts. A little thrill of sensation sparked from her bosom outward to other more tantalizing places.

*Yes, indeed. I am a wanton.*

They'd indulged in numerous clandestine encounters over the past two weeks. Often, they'd only had time for a swift hug, or a hot mouth pressed to her wrist, accompanied by a wicked smile and his seductive gaze. Other times, they'd linger for blood-scorching kisses, and perhaps his hand stroking her spine or the curve of her throat.

Quinn never went beyond that, as if aware she wasn't the kind of woman who could give herself to a man before vows were exchanged.

As he'd warned, his grandmother was an eccentric but lovely woman with a penchant for outlandish wigs. Yesterday she wore a pink monstrosity adorned with several birds. Today, her two-foot-high white wig sported a birdcage. 'Twas a wonder the woman didn't topple over, such were the height and weight of her headdresses.

Nonetheless, Elspet Dunwoodie possessed a keen wit, a charming sense of humor—much like her grandson—and a merry twinkle illuminated her dark brown eyes. Quizzing glass in hand, she'd taken Skye's measure before declaring, "She'll do, my boy. Indeed, she will."

Rising to her toes, Skye kissed his jaw. "Have you spoken with Liam again?"

"No' since last Wednesday. I thought I'd give him time to see how well we get on together, and to finish his snoopin' about. I've nae doubt his man of business has been pokin' around, verifyin' my claims." Twice more, Quinn had approached her mule-headed cousin and each time, he'd staunchly refused to agree to the match.

Disapproval turned Skye's mouth down at the corners. "He's your friend, for pity's sake, and knows your character. I cannot believe he'd stoop so low."

Quinn merely lifted a shoulder and kissed her temple. "He cares about ye, love, and disna want to make a mistake he'd regret later. He'll find nothin' to forbid the match." He gave her a saucy wink and a rakish grin. "I havena a wife hidden away or wee bairns toddlin' about."

"You'd better not, or I shall allow him to call you out." She slapped his shoulder playfully before laying her cheek against the soft wool of his forest-green coat.

Skye truly approached the end of her patience with Liam. But for the sake of the guests and the plans for the Christmastide festivities, she'd steadfastly relegated her frustration to a fusty corner, determined to enjoy the season despite her disappointment.

She, too, had met with her cousin and calmly, but quite firmly, expressed her desire to wed Quinn straightaway. Liam had listened attentively, a small furl pulling his hawkish brows together, one finger tapping the top of his desk. "I am responsible for ye now, Skye. Such a matter canna be entered into lightly."

"I appreciate that, Liam." His genuine concern

wasn't easily dismissed. "But I love him, and he loves me. We have almost from the moment we met. And I believe you can understand how powerful true love is. It changes people. Makes them do things they'd vowed never to do. Makes them better. You, above all people, should know that."

After losing his wife and children in a coaching accident, he'd sworn to never marry again. Skye didn't know the particulars—only that his wife had been a difficult woman and had given him the scar slashing his right cheek.

But then, he'd rescued Emeline from certain death, and despite his pledge to never give his heart again, he'd fallen in love with her. The transformation in him astounded and touched her heart.

Genuine, sacrificial, unconditional love wasn't meant to be disregarded. Rather the opposite. It should be greedily seized and treasured for all time.

"I have an appointment with him in half an hour. That's why I sought ye. He may refuse me again, my love." He caressed her cheek with the back of his hand with such tenderness in his eyes that she wanted to weep.

"He may, but I'm more hopeful." She smoothed his collar. "He's been surreptitiously observing us these past few days. He follows us with his gaze, a pensive expression on his face. I also know Emeline and Aunt Louisa have spoken with him on our behalf as well."

"'Tis good to ken we have their support. We have until Twelfth Night ends before we are forced to make a decision. I canna stay as a guest here forever, Skye." He brushed his fingertips up and down her spine in a soothing fashion. "Ye ken that. I have my own home that I want ye mistress of."

She laid her fingertips on his lips. "Let's not make any rash decisions yet. Christmas is a time of miracles, after all. And convincing my guardian to consent to our nuptials shouldn't be too terribly hard."

He gave her a dubious look and, after scanning the corridor to assure they were alone, tilted her chin with two fingers. Dragonflies capered behind her ribs as he captured her mouth in a fierce, sizzling kiss.

Several delicious, bone-melting minutes passed before she finally, reluctantly drew away. Someday, there'd be no need to end such a blood-stirring kiss.

"You'd best not be late," she urged. "We want to keep his favor. Besides, I need to check with Cook."

"I expect to be on yer team for charades tonight," he said with a whimsical grin. "I quite loathe the game, but I've been informed I canna have any sugar plums or orange puddin' if I dinna cooperate. Kendra MacKay is an honest-to-God fire-breathin' dragon when it comes to her party novelties."

She was, indeed.

He scratched his temple, making him appear quite boyish. "I've been given to understand that all of the hints must have a Christmas theme."

"That's correct." Skye nodded, still uncertain what her clue would be. "Kendra has quite gotten into the Christmas spirit, has she not?"

"She has, indeed," he replied distractedly. Likely, he was pondering what course to take with Liam next to best convince the man that he and Skye should wed.

Quinn drew her into his arms, pressing her head against his chest. "I love ye." He spoke into her hair, giving her shoulders a firm squeeze.

Smiling, her heart overflowing with love for this marvelous man, she tilted her head up. "And I love you. Never forget that. As long as we have each other, we can overcome any obstacle."

A footstep echoed, and he stepped away. An undefinable smile arcing his molded mouth, he retreated down the passageway.

Her heart was so full that she wanted to kick her heels together and dance a jig, Skye watched until he disappeared around the corner.

Though she missed her parents dreadfully, these past two weeks of gaiety and holiday preparations had taken the edge off that pain. And knowing Quinn loved her... Well, no mere words were adequate to express how joyful that made her feel.

She continued to the kitchen and met with Mrs. Spence as planned. Typically, the mistress of the house attended to such matters, but since there were several dishes and special desserts on the extended menu, Emeline invited Skye to speak directly to the cook.

She closed her eyes and sniffed, inhaling the wonderful scents of cinnamon, nutmeg, cloves, ginger, and the other delicious smells that accompanied holiday food preparation. Opening her eyes, she offered Mrs. Spence an approving grin. "I could sit here and breathe in this sumptuousness all day. You've truly outdone yourself."

Mrs. Spence returned Skye's smile with a slightly crooked-tooth grin of her own. "Och, I'm always up for learnin' new recipes, and 'tis been a long while since we had a house full of guests that I could impress with my cookin'." She winked as she stirred a pot.

All sorts of biscuits, gingerbread, and other dainties lay atop one long table beneath a spotless window. The kitchen staff had been very busy helping ensure the holiday would be a success.

"Well, I'm truly most grateful," Skye said. "I cannot tell you how much it means to celebrate Christmas with traditions my mother and father always included." She put her hands on her hips and glanced around the bustling kitchen. "And, I confess, it's been a lot of fun introducing some of the customs here. I must dress for dinner now. Please let me know if there's anything you need."

"Och, lass, I surely will, but I think I've everythin' well in hand." Mrs. Spence angled her chins toward the main house. "Ye just enjoy yerself."

Everything was nearly perfect.

Now if only Liam would agree to permit her and Quinn to wed, Skye could count this as the most joyous Christmas ever.

## 11

The gentleman didn't linger over their port and brandy after supper but, instead, as the last course was cleared away, everyone passed through to the drawing room eager for the evening's entertainment.

More accurately, the married gentlemen were eager to keep their ladies' favor and good-naturedly agreed to eschew the usual after dinner separation of the sexes to indulge their wives.

No doubt, they'd be duly rewarded for their sacrifices, damned lucky buggers.

Quinn, on the other hand, wouldn't be sampling any of Skye's voluptuous charms anytime soon, given the less than successful outcome of his meeting with Liam this afternoon.

Friend or not, he was quite out of patience with Skye's cousin.

As he regarded Liam and Emeline, Logan and Mayra Rutherford, Graeme and Berget Kennedy, and Coburn and Arieen Wallace, also obviously in love, Quinn couldn't help but feel a tiny jolt of envy. How so many of his set had found women who perfectly complemented them was against all odds.

If he didn't miss his mark, interest sparked between Marjorie Kennedy and Roxdale as well. A whole different kind of fire simmered between Kendra and Broden McGregor, however. They'd sniped at each other all evening to the point that the dowager baroness had ordered Kendra to sit beside her on the divan so she could monitor her daughter's behavior.

Arriving for dinner attired in a stunning crimson and black gown, Skye had sucked every bit of air from his lungs. *My God, she is stunnin'.* The rubies at her ears and throat, as well as the bracelet at her wrist, caught the candlelight, glinting like miniature fire stones.

She was, in a word, breathtaking.

His jaw had sagged, and Broden had nudged him in the arm. "Close yer mouth, mon. Ye're gawpin' like a codfish."

Taking a quick sip of his pre-supper drink, he'd covered his gaucheness but had been unable to haul his attention from her for more than a minute or two all evening.

Emeline clapped her hands. "We'll pick the charade teams now. Kendra will pass by with a bowl. Inside are slips of paper that say either *Team 1* or *Team 2*." She arched a winged brow in artificial chastisement. "Nae switchin' either," she admonished, shaking her finger as if they were children in the school room.

Several chuckles greeted her mock scolding.

In short order, the teams had been picked. To Quinn's disappointment, he and Skye weren't on the same side. He gave Liam a sour look from beneath hooded eyes, wondering if it had been by chance or design.

Of course, it was by chance.

Everyone had picked from the same bowl. He was

just out of sorts and his continued disappointment was taking a toll.

Skye cast him an apologetic smile and, with the epitome of feminine grace, glided to sit with her team.

"I'm quite good at charades," Grandmother announced as she settled into an armchair and regally nodded her head. This evening's wig, a rather conservative head covering compared to her earlier flamboyant hair dressings—was only adorned with green and gold silk flowers, ribbons, and feathers to match her gown.

She was having the time of her life, and gratitude for permitting her to be included in the house party tapped behind his ribs. She also heartily approved of Skye.

Everyone had written their Christmastide subject for the charades on slips of paper prior to dinner and placed them in another cut-crystal bowl. Emeline quickly explained the rules for those who hadn't played before, and amid much hilarity, groans, laughter and cries of, "No' done," or "Ye canna talk," over an hour passed.

"'Tis yer turn, Liam," his wife said sweetly, crossing to present him with the bowl containing only a few scraps of paper.

Quinn stifled a chuckle.

Liam wasn't long on parlor games.

Leveling his wife a long-suffering look, he unfolded his arms and straightened from where he'd been leaning beside the fireplace. With a theatrical sigh that would've earned Shakespeare's applause, he reached inside the bowl and withdrew a neatly folded piece of paper.

"Mayhap ye drew holly," Quinn suggested with false solicitousness. "Ye're prickly already, so we should be able to guess quickly."

Liam eyed Quinn's ill-concealed smirk. "Need I remind ye, that ye havena taken a turn either?"

True. They were on the same side and on the opposite team, only Berget and Marjorie Kennedy had yet to demonstrate their acting skills.

"We're to have mulled cider when we're done." Skye swept her gaze around the room. "And wassail as well."

The old light had returned to her mesmerizing blue eyes and the healthy glow to her cheeks. This distraction was precisely what she'd needed.

"I am so glad you suggested this gathering," Marjorie Kennedy said. "I've missed celebrating Christmas."

"Let's have at it then." Liam turned another undiscernible glance on Quinn.

He'd done that often of late, and Quinn had begun to consider that he might've overstayed his welcome. Would he be asked to leave when the festivities ended?

By thunder, he'd not be leaving without his beloved Skye.

Liam cleared his throat, brushing his hand through his hair. He swiftly perused the slip of paper, then wadded it into a tight little ball and tossed it in the fire.

Emeline gave him an encouraging little nudge and directed what could only be called a secretive smile toward Skye.

Quinn looked between Liam and his wife.

What were they about?

His discussion with Liam this afternoon had gone

better than expected. He hadn't committed to allowing Quinn to marry Skye. However, this time, he hadn't said no outright either.

"I'm considerin' yer request," Liam had said with his usual severity. Clapping a hand on his nape, he cleared his throat again.

He raised four fingers.

"Four words," Broden said.

Liam nodded and held up one finger.

"First word," Dowager Baroness Penderhaven said, a rather surprising competitive gleam in her eyes, so like her son's and daughter's. She exchanged a conspiratorial glance with Quinn's grandmother who leaned forward a bit in anticipation.

He pointed to his eye.

"Eye. I?" Bethea Glanville cried, glancing around for approval.

Nodding again, Liam displayed two fingers.

"Second word," Grandmother announced unnecessarily.

A combination of chagrin and concentration lining his face, he made a pushing motion.

"Shove."

"Push."

"Thrust."

"Heave?"

At the wild guesses, he harrumphed and pretended to shape a square box and offer it to Quinn.

"We have to remember the clues are all Christmas-themed," Skye reminded them.

"Och, well, I dinna much like havin' to portray the arse Mary sat upon," Graeme Kennedy grumbled.

Everyone burst out laughing.

Liam emphasized the shape of a square package again.

"Present?" Berget suggested.

Marjorie Kennedy said, "Gift. That's Christmas-themed."

"Offering?" Quinn's grandmother put in.

Liam rolled his eyes ceilingward, a muscle in his jaw beginning to tic. He motioned emphatically from his chest to Quinn several times.

"Bosoms?" Boden dared drolly, earning him a blistering glower from Kendra.

Confused frowns and shrugs met Liam's evermore terse gestures.

"Oh, I think I know." Skye waved her hand. "Give?"

A grin split Liam's face, and a flush of pleasure skimmed her face at her cleverness.

"All right, we have *I give* so far," Coburn Wallace murmured.

Holding up three fingers, Liam pointed at Quinn.

"What in the world?" The dowager baroness appeared completely lost. "I give *Quinn*? Does it sound like Quinn?"

The others all began talking at once.

"Fin?"

"Sin?"

"Twin?"

"Spin?"

Liam gesticulated harder.

"Thin?"

"Tin?"

"Kin?"

"Shin?"

"Gin?"

"Grin?"

"Chin?"

Releasing a loud, frustrated snort, Liam pointed at himself as he vigorously shook his head back and forth. He pointed his finger at Quinn and then everyone else and nodded like a lunatic or a drunkard.

"Liam, my friend, ye're dismal at this game." Logan chuckled and received a thunderous scowl in return.

*I give…give what?*

Quinn flexed his eyes the merest bit, trying to pay attention, but he couldn't keep his gaze off of Skye's radiant face. She was having such a splendid time.

*Ye.*

All at once Quinn knew.

*I give ye…permission.*

He jerked his head up and met Liam's gray gaze, a question in his own. He cut Skye a sideways glance, then flicked his attention back to Liam.

Liam gave the merest flex of his eyes and dip of his chin.

"I give ye permission," Quinn said softly, reverently. Almost unable to believe the truth of the words. He had permission to marry his cherished Skye.

"Oohh," Grandmother breathed, unfurling her ostrich feather fan and waving it furiously before her face as she blinked just as rapidly.

"Aye." Liam slapped him on the shoulder.

"Badly done,." Kendra objected, giving Quinn a gimlet glare. "Quinn, ye solved it for them. How does that work for the scorekeepin'? And what in the world does that have to do with Christmastide?" She wrinkled her nose. "Logan is correct. Ye're absolutely horrid at charades, Liam."

"Shh, my dear. I dinna believe the game's up quite yet," her mother said, smiling from ear to ear.

The room gradually grew silent; quite a feat considering how many people were present. But it was as if everyone at once became aware that something more monumental than a nonsensical charade had taken place.

Quinn pulled his coat straight and took the five short steps to where Skye sat.

She cut her puzzled gaze behind him to Liam and then back to Quinn.

Dropping to one knee, he gathered her hand in his.

Her mouth parted into a startled "O".

Understanding swept over her face. Joy lit her eyes and a smile so luminous curved her face, as if the sun had entered the room in all its incandescent glory.

A collective gasp went up from the ladies, and the men made approving sounds in their throats.

"Skye, my love. Will ye marry this humble man so unworthy of ye but who loves ye more than mortal words can say?"

Bobbing her head excitedly, the feathers in her wig threatening to take flight, Grandmother pointed her fan at Skye. "Yes. Yes. Oh, do say yes, my dear."

"Yes, yes." Tears glistened in Skye's azure eyes. She nodded so enthusiastically that two silky blonde curls escaped their pins and bounced to her nape. "I shall marry you."

As everyone applauded, he pressed his mouth to the back of her hand. "Thank ye, my love."

"I do believe that's quite the most romantic thing

I've ever seen." The dowager baroness dabbed daintily at her eyes.

"Liam, I amend my earlier comment about how horrid ye are at charades," Logan said. "That was brilliant."

"This calls for a toast," Graeme Kennedy announced. "Didna I hear somethin' about mulled cider and wassail earlier?"

"Indeed, ye did." Emeline swept to the bell pull.

Quinn stood, gently drawing Skye to her feet.

She still appeared half-dazed.

He well knew the feeling.

"You didn't tell me he gave his permission," she said quietly, her words muffled in all the well wishes and good cheer.

He leaned closer, speaking into her dainty ear. "He didna. He only said he wouldna say nae. I kent nothin' about this." He circled his hand in the air.

In short order, everyone had a beverage of choice in hand, and Liam raised his glass. "To Quinn and Skye. May their happiness and joy be as vast as the ocean, and their troubles and sorrows as light as thistledown."

Tucking Skye to his side, Quinn drew her away from the others until they stood near the relative privacy of the window nook. Holding her hand, he took a swallow of the mulled wine. "Och, that's a fine brew." He lifted the cup, taking a deep breath of the aromatic mixtures. "I could well become accustomed to this."

"It does warm one through and through." She took a dainty sip.

"When do ye want to exchange vows, my love?" Pray God she didn't want a long betrothal.

"Would tomorrow be too soon?" she quipped.

"No' for me."

She sobered, considering him from beneath her lashes.

"If you've no objections, I'd truly like to wed Christmas morning. I know it's not entirely proper, considering I'm in mourning. But I feel in my heart that it's right. I know my parents wouldn't have objected if they were alive." She gave his forearm an excited little squeeze. "We can begin our new life together as our friends are celebrating new-to-them

Twelfth Night traditions, and we also commemorate Christ's birth. What could be more perfect?"

"Nothin', my heart." Clearing his throat, he glanced around the room. "May I have yer attention?"

Once more, the drawing room settled into respectful silence.

He gathered Skye's hand in his, smiling into her shining face. "Ye came to celebrate the Christmas holiday, but Skye and I would be honored if ye'd also attend our weddin' on Christmas morn."

## Epilogue

Snow had fallen overnight, cloaking the frozen Highlands in a shimmering, pristine blanket.

Utterly perfect for Christmas.

Even more perfect for Skye's wedding day. Her tummy tumbled over itself as Kendra finished arranging her hair. She tucked in a sprig of holly and ivy before standing back and admiring her handiwork.

"Beautiful," Kendra pronounced. "Never has there been a more stunnin' Christmas bride."

Her eyes misty with emotion, Skye stood and hugged her cousin.

"Yer mother and father would be so proud, Skye." Aunt Louisa blinked rapidly, a watery smile bending her mouth. "And so verra pleased to see ye this happy."

"I am happy." Blissfully so.

Only a few short weeks ago, she'd wondered if she'd ever know contentment again, and now she knew a joy far beyond anything she might've conjured in her imagination. Because Quinn loved her.

How appropriate during this season when the Christians around the world acknowledged the love and sacrifice of their Savior that she should find her way back from the darkness that had threatened to engulf her. Because of the gift of love Quinn had given her.

Never would she underestimate the power of love again. *Never.*

She kissed her aunt's soft cheek. "Thank you for everything. I don't know how I would have managed without you."

"'Tis been a pleasure, my dear."

Shaking out the folds of her gown, Skye brushed a slightly trembling hand over her elaborately embroidered stomacher as the crimson fabric settled around her feet. Her silk square-toed, ruby-colored shoes peaked from beneath the hem of the same gown she'd been wearing when Quinn proposed.

The finest frock she owned, other than her ballgowns, it seemed most fitting to wed the man she adored above all else in the whole of the entire world in the gown she'd accepted his proposal in. She wore the same ruby jewels she'd worn the other night, as well as a magnificent diamond, pearl, and ruby Luckenbooth brooch.

Her betrothal and Christmas gift from Quinn.

He couldn't wait until later when the others opened their gifts to present it to her. He'd wanted her to wear the token of his affection during the ceremony.

Naturally, she readily complied.

She could deny him nothing.

Twenty minutes later, she stood outside the drawing room, her previous nerves having abated. Instead, a surreal calmness enveloped her at the rightness of what she was about to do. She and Quinn were destined to be together. She'd known that since he strode into the drawing room that fateful day and his spirit had touched hers across the space.

Liam, looking ever so dashing in a cobalt velvet

suit, waited to escort her inside.

Emeline and Kendra, acting as her attendants and each with a bouquet of holiday greenery, were positioned near the three-sided window nook.

Broden McGregor stood beside Quinn, but his gaze flicked to Kendra every so often. An enigmatic expression would flit across his rugged features, only to vanish a second later, giving Skye reason to ponder if he was truly as off put by her as he proclaimed.

Quinn smiled at Skye, and her blood sang with happiness.

Her pulse quickened as she took in his somber black suit and his golden-brown hair neatly brushed. He presented quite the most wonderful sight for a young bride. He would be her husband soon, joy of joys.

She examined the festive room, now filled with smiling houseguests.

Wearing an *a la Grecque* styled wig, Mrs. Dunwoodie sat beside Aunt Louisa.

Skye sincerely hoped Emeline and Liam considered making the Christmas gathering an annual event.

Would she be minutes away from becoming Quinn's wife if she hadn't dared to ask for a Christmas celebration? Had the holiday worked its magic on Liam and persuaded him to allow the match. Or had other, more powerful forces been at work?

She had no way of knowing, of course, and it didn't matter. In a few minutes, she'd be Mrs. Quinn Catherwood. Skye Catherwood, the happiest woman on earth.

Liam approached and gave her a gentle smile. "Ye have nae doubts, lass? If ye do, I can call the weddin' off with a single word."

She placed her palm on his forearm and clasped her other hand more firmly around the ribbon-wrapped stems of her bouquet. "I've never been more certain of anything in my life."

The string quartet struck their first chords and, taking a deep breath, she allowed her cousin to guide her to her groom.

Liam took his position beside Broden, and the cleric cleared his throat.

She couldn't drag her attention from the wonderment and adoration on Quinn's face. She must've answered the questions put to her, but the ceremony passed in a fog.

*I'm marrying Quinn*

*Christmas wishes do come true.*

Then Quinn was smiling, his eyes suspiciously moist, and applause resounded behind her. She blinked, coming out of her daze as he bent to brush his mouth over hers. "I love ye, *leannan*."

He started to lift his head, but Skye clasped his nape, giving him a naughty smile. "Oh, I think you can do better than that, Quinn."

A delighted matronly chuckle echoed behind her. "She'll keep my grandson on his toes, to be sure."

Bedevilment glittered in his pale green eyes, and he scooped her against him. "Does my lady bride wish a Christmas kiss from her Highland groom?"

"Oh, she does. She does."

And to her delight, and no doubt the astonishment of those looking on, he proceeded to kiss her most ardently and thoroughly.

"Happy Christmas, darlin," he whispered.

Laughing, Skye cupped his cheek. "Happy life, my love."

# About the Author

*USA Today* Bestselling, award-winning author COLLETTE CAMERON® scribbles Scottish and Regency historicals featuring dashing rogues and scoundrels and the intrepid damsels who reform them.Blessed with an overactive and witty muse that won't stop whispering new romantic romps in her ear, she's lived in Oregon her entire life, though she dreams of living in Scotland part-time. A self-confessed Cadbury chocoholic, you'll always find a dash of inspiration and a pinch of humor in her sweet-to-spicy timeless romances®.

Explore **Collette's worlds** at
www.collettecameron.com!

Join her **VIP Reader Club** and **FREE newsletter**.
Giggles guaranteed!

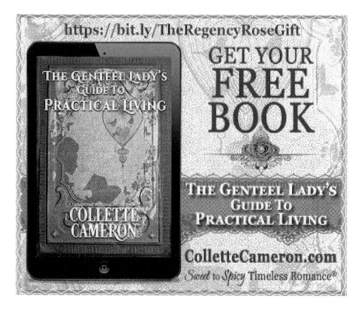

**FREE BOOK:** Join Collette's The Regency Rose®
VIP Reader Club to get updates on book releases,
cover reveals, contests, and giveaways she reserves
exclusively for email and newsletter followers. Also,
any deals, sales, or special promotions are offered to
club members first. She will not share your name or
email, nor will she spam you.

http://bit.ly/TheRegencyRoseGift

**Follow Collette on BookBub**
https://www.bookbub.com/authors/collette-cameron

As always when researching for my stories, I learned several fun facts pertaining to Christmas in Scotland and England during the early 18th century that I wanted to share with you. As I mentioned in A CHRISTMAS KISS FOR THE HIGHLANDER, Christmas and Yule weren't openly celebrated in Scotland.

Late in the 16th century, St. Mungo's Cathedral wished to abolish the pagan rituals associated with Yule (originally the Viking festival *jól*) and the Kirk threatened excommunication for anyone caught participating in Yule. In 1640, an Act of Parliament made Yule illegal, and the intolerance was taken a step further when an ordinance passed (supported by Oliver Cromwell) that banned the feast of Christmas as well. Several sources record that during that same time period, he also forbade the eating of pie.

Those are fighting words! I adore pie.

Though the ordinances and laws were repealed a few years later, the Church still frowned upon the celebration of Yule and Christmas. Hence, most Scots didn't openly celebrate the holiday until 1958. Another interesting tidbit I uncovered was that Christmas was outlawed in Boston, Massachusetts from 1659 to 1681.

My research regarding clove oranges also proved quite fascinating. Pomander balls date back to as early as the mid-thirteenth century. However, the clove orange gained popularity in the 17th and 18th centuries.

I used to make them myself as a child.

To stay within the bounds of historical accuracy as much as possible, I researched the origins of sugar plums and gingerbread. First mentioned in literature in the 16<sup>th</sup> century, sugar plums are not sugar-coated plums but comfits. A comfit is a sort of sweet with a sugar shell around a center, often an almond.

I was delighted with what I learned about gingerbread. The very first recipe for gingerbread is attributed to the Greeks over two thousand years before the birth of Christ. A European version was developed by the late Middle Ages. However, lavish decorated gingerbread is attributed to Queen Elizabeth I. These cookies were decorated with gold leaf.

Finally, in order to embellish Eytone Hall with holiday greenery and to allow the ladies to make kissing boughs, I needed to snoop around a bit to see precisely what types of greenery grew in the Highlands or Midlands in 1720. I was delighted to discover holly was a native plant to Scotland, and although mistletoe isn't common, it can be found. Other greens such as pine boughs, rosemary, and ivy were all easily accessible to decorate with as well.

I had so much fun researching and writing A CHRISTMAS KISS FOR THE HIGHLANDER and hope you enjoyed reading Quinn and Skye's romance. If so, please consider leaving a review. I'd appreciate it very much! Be sure to check out the other books in my HEART OF A SCOT series too.

To make sure you don't miss any of my book news, subscribe to The Regency Rose, my newsletter

(Get a free book too!). I also have a fabulous VIP Reader Group on Facebook. If you're a fan of my books and historical romance, I'd love to have you join me. You'll also be the first to see new covers, read exclusive excerpts, be the first to know about contests and giveaways, help me pick titles and name characters, and much, much more.

Please consider telling other readers why you enjoyed this book by reviewing it as well. I also truly adore hearing from my readers. You can contact me on my website and while you are there, explore my author world.

Hugs,

Collette

**Connect with Collette!**

*Check out her author world:*
collettecameron.com
*Join her Reader Group:*
www.facebook.com/groups/CollettesCheris
*Subscribe to her newsletter, receive a FREE Book:*
www.signup.collettecameron.com/TheRegencyRoseGift

# Triumph and Treasure

Highland Heather Romancing a Scot Series, Book One

**She was a means to an end…**

**he wasn't supposed to ever love her.**

*He lived an idyllic life…*

One day, Flynn, Earl of Luxmoore, was a wealthy, carefree lord, courting the woman he intended to wed. And the next day, he's stripped of all but his title and left with no means to care for his loved ones. When the person responsible for his ruination offers him a solution—marriage to an unwilling and resentful American beauty—he has no choice but to accept. Not if he wants to care for his ailing mother, elderly grandmother, and disabled sister.

*Fate dealt her a cruel hand…*

Angelina Ellsworth unwittingly committed bigamy, and when she finds herself pregnant, she'll do anything to protect her baby. Including fleeing to England and marrying a handsome nobleman, every bit as desperate and opposed to their marriage of convenience as she. She agrees to wed Flynn, stipulating two conditions: the union is in name only, and after a year, they'll go their separate ways. Except, Angelina didn't count on her first husband, refusing to let her go.

***Resentment and anger war with passion and desire…***
Flynn risks his life to protect Angelina from the madman pursuing her, but is his sacrifice enough? Can a woman who's vowed to never trust a man again and an embittered lord find contentment in an arranged marriage neither wanted?

CPSIA information can be obtained
at www.ICGtesting.com
Printed in the USA
LVHW082131091121
702920LV00026B/962

9 781954 307858